"Philippe, what makes you think I haven't already moved on mentally and emotionally? You're wading into some seriously unknown territory here."

He didn't answer right away. Instead he extended his index finger and put it behind her ear. He was barely touching her as he ran his finger down her neck. Her breathing changed almost imperceptibly; only someone who knew her as well as he did could have heard the tiny sigh that escaped her lips. She leaned toward him and put her hand on his waist while he slowly drew her into his arms. When she was so close that they could feel each other's heartbeat, he bent his head to hers until their lips touched.

Philippe's mouth touched hers gently at first, but their mutual consent to the embrace signaled more. Chastain opened her mouth slightly, enough to run her tongue along his lower lip and gently pull it into her mouth, while he did the same to her upper lip. The tentative tasting turned into a long, sensual exploration that showed no sign of ending. They kissed until they were devouring each other, trying to satisfy the hungry desire that had been aroused.

"This is how I know we aren't finished, Chastain. Will you stay with me for Christmas?"

A voice she barely recognized answered him. "Yes."

Books by Melanie Schuster

Kimani Romance

Working Man
Model Perfect Passion
Trust in Me
A Case for Romance
Picture Perfect Christmas

Kimani Arabesque

Lucky in Love
Candlelight and You
Until the End of Time
My One and Only Love
Let it Be Me
A Merry Little Christmas
Something to Talk About
A Fool for You
Chain of Fools
The Closer I Get to You

MELANIE SCHUSTER

started reading when she was four and believes that's why she's a writer today. She was always fascinated with books, loved telling stories and always wanted to be a writer. She fell in love with romance novels when she began reading the ones her mother would bring home. She would go to any store that sold paperbacks and load up! Whenever Melanie had a spare moment she was reading. She loves romance fiction because it's always so hopeful. Despite the harsh realities of life, romance stories always remind readers of the wonderful, exciting adventure of falling in love and meeting your soul mate. Melanie finds fulfillment in writing stories about compelling couples who find true, lasting love in the face of all obstacles. She hopes all of her readers find true love. And if they've already been lucky enough to find love, she hopes that they never forget what it felt like to fall in love.

PICTURE
PERFECT
Christmas

MELANIE SCHUSTER

KIMANI™
ROMANCE

To Malachi Jabari McCray, a true warrior and a fighter.
Never give up.

And to my very creative and supportive editor,
Evette Porter. Thanks for your patience!

 KIMANI PRESS™

ISBN-13: 978-0-373-86138-5

PICTURE PERFECT CHRISTMAS

Copyright © 2009 by Melanie Schuster

Recycling programs
for this product may
not exist in your area.

www.kimanipress.com

Printed in U.S.A.

Dear Reader,

So many of you have been asking for another Deveraux story, so this is my holiday gift to you all! I love stories about couples who get back together after a long separation and that's the case with Chastain and Philippe.

Thanks for going with me on another journey with the Deveraux, and look for another story in the not-too-distant future. Wade Deveraux is still single but he's going to get knocked for a loop by love!

Happy holidays with love,

Melanie

I *Chronicles* 4:10

Acknowledgments

My heartfelt and sincere thanks go out to
Dr. Mark Adams and his wonderful staff for getting
me back on my feet again. And thanks to all my
family, friends, and readers who have supported me
and encouraged me and put up with me, especially my
online family.

To my sister in Christ, Betty, no words can express my
gratitude for our friendship.

And to Jamil, my play brother and my friend, thanks
for always believing in me.

Chapter 1

New York City

Pale sunlight streamed through the huge windows of the gallery. Chastain Thibodaux looked at the winter sky and frowned. "I don't know why the sun bothers to shine when it's this cold," she said grumpily. Her assistant, Mona Morgan, was checking the order of the paintings that were waiting to be hung. She looked up from her clipboard and laughed.

"You act like it's never cold in France. We had lots of cold weather there as you well know. Snow and all."

Chastain sat down on a stool that was near the entrance. "Yes, but it was *French* snow. Very chic, *chérie*. Lulu looked fabulous in her little red coat, didn't you?" she said, directing her remark to her West Highland white terrier that was busily sniffing every corner of the gallery.

"And she'll look just as cute right here in Harlem," Mona replied. "You're not sorry that you left Paris, are you?"

Chastain looked away pensively before she answered. "No. Three years was enough. I loved living in Europe, but I was ready to come home. I missed my family and I missed the States. I had an absentee ballot. But imagine what it would have been like being here for the presidential election," she said. "We missed so much being in Europe while the election was taking place. Seeing it on TV wasn't the same. I must admit that President Obama's election is one of the reasons I was so glad to come back. And I loved living in New York when I was here before. It's one of my favorite places in the world besides N'awlins." She looked out the window at the pale sun again. "I just wish it was spring already."

"Are you crazy? Christmas in New York is like a fantasy! This is the best time of year to be here," Mona protested.

"If you say so. Just wait until you're trying to get home during rush hour and your feet are soaking wet and freezing and you can't get a cab to save your life. Then see how swell it is." Chastain stood up and stretched her body like a cat. "But I'm not going to lie. I do love this city."

"Then I'll have to make you want to stay forever."

David Llewellyn's voice interrupted their conversation from the back of the gallery. The owner of the art gallery, he was tall, dark and very handsome. He had been one of Chastain's professors in graduate school and they'd been close friends ever since. When her three-year fellowship ended, he'd urged her to come to New York and have her first big showing at Studio L, his highly regarded gallery in Harlem.

Chastain gave him a sweet smile. "Make me want to stay forever? How do you plan to do that?"

He was standing in front of her and returned her smile with one of his own that made him even more handsome. With his dimples showing, he leaned down and kissed her cheek. "I can't tell you. But I can show you if you give me a chance."

Whatever flirtatious answer she was about to give vanished as Lulu lunged at David. She stood up and barked to get his attention, which made him laugh. "First thing on my list is to make friends with your dog. Isn't that the way to get to your mistress, little girl?"

Chastain and Mona rolled their eyes. "You don't have to charm her, David. Lulu's a sucker for men, all men. She's been following your manager around all morning. Just a regular little trollop, if you ask me," Mona said. "Get your leash and I'll take you for a walk, Lulu."

Lulu dashed off and brought back the leash, but she dropped it on David's feet and looked up at him with love in her eyes.

"See? A total trollop," Mona said fondly.

"Well, how can I resist such a delightful invitation? I'll take her for a stroll and then I'll take you to lunch. How does that sound?"

"Perfect," Chastain answered. "As long as we can go to that chicken and waffles place."

Mona watched David and Lulu leave, and then she turned to Chastain. "You've been holding out on me," she said in a low voice. Veronica, the gallery's receptionist, was within earshot and Mona was trying to be discreet.

Chastain looked at her with amusement. "I have no idea what you're talking about. Come on upstairs with me."

Once they were safely out of earshot of Veronica, the sales staff and the manager of the gallery, James Steffney, Mona chided her boss.

"You've been holding out on me. I just got a really good look at Mr. David Llewellyn and he's much better looking than any professor I ever met, so drop the act. He's your new man, isn't he?"

Chastain had to laugh. She almost hated to disappoint Mona, but the truth was just not that interesting.

"Girl, you are obsessed! You're worse than my BFF Paris Deveraux who's the biggest matchmaker I know. I told you, he was my professor and mentor when I was working on my master's. We became good friends, nothing else. When he came to France last year he invited me to have a showing here in New York when I finished my project. So don't go reading more into the situation than there is," Chastain said pointedly.

Mona pushed her long, curly hair behind one ear. "I hear what you're saying, but I also see how he looks at you. I also hear how he talks to you. And trust me, none of my *friends* react to me like that. He gave us this upstairs apartment to live in while we're here, and as far as I know that's very unusual. That place could rent for a few thou a month, easy. Doesn't that seem a little more than *friendly* to you?"

"I'm going to ignore you," Chastain replied. "Give your overactive imagination a rest," she added as she headed toward the bedroom.

"You can run, but you can't hide," Mona shouted after her. "I won't be denied vital information. Inquiring minds have to know."

Chastain shook her head. She would admit that lending her the apartment was extra nice of David. It was a beautiful space that was furnished like a design show house. The furniture was mid-century modern and the colors were soft neutrals with pops of bright color. It was extremely generous of David to suggest that she and Mona stay there while her work was being shown, especially since it would go from December 1 through the end of February.

She went into the large bathroom and surveyed herself in the mirror on the wall behind the counter. Turning on the faucet above the clear glass bowl pedestal sink, she quickly brushed her teeth and washed her hands, then patted her face with a damp washcloth. After working all morning, she should have been at least slightly disheveled, but she was immaculate, as always. She was wearing black wool Capri pants, black ballet slippers and a bronze cashmere cardigan trimmed with little copper beads. She had the sweater on backward so the V-neck showed off an enticing but modest glimpse of her back. She changed into long pants and ankle boots because of the cold weather. Growing up in New Orleans, she enjoyed the chilly temperatures but she never quite adjusted to them.

She heard the sound of the elevator descending to the first floor. David was coming upstairs to deliver Lulu and collect Chastain.

Mona waved at her and said, "Bring me a doggie bag, please."

"Don't be ridiculous. You're coming, too."

"Chastain, here's your baby safe and sound," David said. "She was a perfect lady on our walk."

"Were you a good girl? Then you get a treat." Lulu ran to her crate and was waiting for her when she came in with Pup-peronis in hand.

"I'll be back soon," Chastain promised. She got her coat and joined David and Mona in the living room. "Okay, David, I think we're ready to go. I'm famished."

In a short while they were seated in Sylvia's Restaurant, one of New York's soul food landmarks. Chastain knew she wouldn't have any complaints about the food at Sylvia's. She had eaten there many times in the past. Mona was sipping sweet tea and looking around appreciatively. Chastain was sticking to hot coffee, insisting that she needed the warmth.

David looked at Mona appraisingly. "So are you related to Chastain?" he asked.

Both women shook their heads. "I have about nine thousand cousins, but Monie isn't one of them. And I'm an only child, remember?"

"Of course I do. Believe it or not, I remember everything you've ever shared with me," he said smoothly. "But I don't think you told me how you two met."

Chastain winced as she felt a little kick from Mona under the table. She ignored it and began speaking. "We met at a Biedermeier exhibit at the Louvre. Then we kept bumping into each other at different galleries and she took a class that I was teaching and that's how we became friends. So when you made the generous offer to show my paintings, I needed an assistant and she volunteered to help," Chastain added.

"Volunteered? *Stalked* is more like it. I followed her around, brought her coffee and croissants, and made a pest of myself until she said she would hire me. I had just finished my studies at Sorbonne and I needed a break. So I'm working for a while until I decide whether to get a doctorate or a job," Mona said cheerfully. "And the only other alternative was to go back to D.C. and be my father's hostess until I could prove I could support myself, so I am totally happy. I love my dad, but a woman's got to be on her own sometime," she added.

The subject changed when the food arrived. "Are you ready for your interview tomorrow?" David asked.

Chastain made a little face. "Yes, I am. I'm still not

sure why anybody wants to interview me, but I'm game."

David had contacts everywhere and Chastain was booked for radio, newspaper and magazine interviews. She'd been interviewed before, when she won the fellowship that sent her to Paris, and in fact had very favorable press coverage while she was there. It was David's opinion that she was a natural in front of the camera and the microphone, and he told her so.

"You're beautiful, brilliant, elegant and thoroughly charming, and anyone who meets you is enriched by the experience. Besides, you're about to blow up in a major way. It's called taking the art world by storm. Just relax and get used to it, Chastain."

When she was younger, Chastain would have turned purple with embarrassment and used her self-deprecating humor to deflect his words. Now she just thanked him in a low, sultry voice that brought another kick from Mona.

They finished their meals with pleasant chitchat and Mona and David watched in amazement while Chastain consumed a large serving of peach cobbler. "Where do you put all that food?" Mona said in consternation. "I'm about a dumpling away from Lane Bryant and you pack it in like a sumo wrestler but you weigh less than a runway model. I could hate you, really I could."

Chastain gave her spoon a sexy little lick. "Genes, honey. All the Thibodauxes are on the skinny side. We have the metabolisms of a hummingbird. Wait until you meet my family, then you'll see what I mean. They're coming up here in a couple of weeks. I hope New York is ready for them because they bring the party with them wherever they go," she said with a wicked grin.

"*Laissez les bon temps rouler,* huh?" David said, chuckling.

"Oh, we let the good times roll like you've never seen in this life," she assured him.

She regaled the table with some of the exploits of her uncles and cousins in the French Quarter where she'd grown up and they were all laughing uproariously when the check came for their meal. "I had an unorthodox childhood, but I wouldn't have traded it for anything," she said.

As she and Mona put their coats on while David took care of the check, she realized that she meant every word. There was a time when she wasn't comfortable with certain aspects of her upbringing, but those days were long past. There was nothing in the world she couldn't handle now. She could hold her head high and meet anyone in the world on an equal footing. Somewhere along the line, she had grown into her own skin and she liked it. No, she deserved it and she was loving every minute of it.

Chapter 2

Chastain stood in the middle of the gallery and looked around in amazement. It was humbling and exhilarating at the same time. All of her works were hung and lit to show every detail of her talent. Everything was ready for the opening and so was she. She was feeling more serene than nervous. She had worked hard for this and she was ready for the next level. David had pulled out all the stops for her showing and she was grateful for his efforts.

Studio L was huge. The walls were covered in oyster-white wool flannel and the floors were covered in taupe Berber carpet. The walls were moveable and could be arranged in any manner to better display artwork and there were stainless steel pillars for sculptures and other kinds of work. There were seating areas here and there but not too many; David wanted to encourage the flow of foot traffic. Tall potted trees graced the corners and added a jolt of natural color to the neutral palette of the room. In the high ceiling, there was a combination of pinpoint halogen lights and some hand-sculpted fixtures in stainless steel that were a perfect counterpoint to the carefully arranged display lights.

For the special invitation-only showing, there was a wine bar and a buffet, catered by Melba's. Any sales from the first week of the showing would go to the continuing restoration of New Orleans, a project that was a passion of Chastain's. The soft music of a live jazz trio and the quiet hum of David's highly efficient staff made it all look like a scene in a movie.

She had to stifle a giggle at the thought. David arrived unobtrusively at her side with a flute of sparkling wine. "What, may I ask, is so funny?"

"I was picturing a scene in an Audrey Hepburn movie, only I was the star," she admitted. "Thanks, but I don't drink, David. Alcohol has had its way with one too many members of the Thibodaux family, so I leave it alone."

"And that's why this is a passionfruit spumante without a drop of alcohol. I told you I pay attention to everything about you," he said as she took the flute.

"You're too good to be true, David. Everything looks beautiful, don't you think?"

"I think you look beautiful," he replied, caressing

her face with his dark eyes. "That ensemble is amazing," he added.

Chastain smoothed the supple silk fabric over her
hip. She was wearing a lustrous gold knee-length dress
with a layered drape that began at the right side of the
waist. The dress's strapless bodice fit her perfectly,
showing off her tiny waist and the straight skirt had a
slit up the back that allowed her to walk easily in her
three-inch slingback gold heels. Her necklace was
made of amber, citrines and topaz set in gold wire
arranged in an abstract pattern, and her matching
earrings were twisted wires with citrine and goldstone
beads.

"Who's the designer?" he asked. "There'll be a lot
of reporters here tonight and someone is bound to ask."

"The dress is vintage Dior. I got it at this fabulous
flea market in Paris. And the jewelry is my design," she
said, fingering the smooth stones. "I made it."

"I told you we should have put some jewelry in the
show," David said. "Women will go wild for that."

Chastain shrugged. "I don't have enough pieces yet.
I only started making jewelry recently and I'm still ex-
perimenting. Besides, I think there's enough on
display, don't you?"

"I'd say there's just the right amount. I have a
feeling those nudes are going to get a lot of attention,"
he said, and they both turned to the centerpiece of the
exhibit. Three life-size oil paintings were displayed in
the center of the room. They were amazingly lifelike.
In fact, the viewer had to get very close to see that they

weren't photographs. All three were of the same model, a man with well-defined muscles who exuded raw sexuality. In one portrait he was bathing, in one he was standing on a balcony and in the third, he was making love to a very lucky woman. The mystery of the pictures was the absence of a clear view of his full face. There was just enough to mesmerize the viewer into a private fantasy about the subject.

"I don't remember you ever painting nudes before," David remarked.

"I did quite a few when I was an undergrad," Chastain said. "You know that drawing figures and painting are required in most art programs. All we did was draw nudes in those classes. There were always a few pervs who tried to audit the class to see the naked models, but they were for art majors only."

David persisted, "That's true, of course. But when I saw your work in Paris I don't remember those. They're not easy to forget."

"No one has ever seen them but me. I painted them after I got to Paris and they weren't for exhibit, they were just for me," she said demurely.

"After tonight that's all going to change, sweetheart. Everybody who sees them is going to love them."

They touched their glasses in a toast and exchanged a brief kiss.

The invitation-only crowd was thoroughly enjoying Chastain's work. She'd met so many new people and received so many compliments that she couldn't help but keep a smile on her face. The champagne was flowing and the excellent jazz made the perfect backdrop for conversation. Mona was at her most sociable, meeting and greeting everyone and handing out Chastain's brochures and business cards. People had approached her with questions about commissioned work and she'd also had many inquiries about her jewelry, once Mona informed several fashionable women that she'd created it. David never strayed too far from her. But he didn't smother her with attention. He was just there if she needed anything. It was truly the most spectacular night she could remember.

She was about to look for a quiet corner to sit and catch her breath when a large hand clasped her upper arm, firmly but gently. A shivery sensation went down her spine and she heard the last voice she expected to hear that night or any other.

"What in the hell do you think you're doing, Chastain? Is this your idea of a joke?"

It was Philippe Deveraux, speaking in a tone that she'd never heard before. Philippe had been many things to her in the past, but he'd never been angry and he'd never embarrassed her in public. She was shocked, jerking away from him while she turned to face him.

"How dare you…" Her voice trailed away as she looked up into a face that didn't belong to the Philippe she'd last known. His long ponytail was gone, replaced by a short, close-cropped haircut. His full beard was now a well-groomed goatee with a mustache and he was wearing a designer suit and expensive leather shoes. She was stunned by the change in him and her face showed it. But she quickly rallied and went right back to telling him off.

"How dare you show up here and get up in my face? What's wrong with you? How did you get in, anyway? This showing is by invitation only," she added haughtily.

James Steffney was the gallery's manager. He looked more like an NFL linebacker than someone who was interested in the pursuit of fine art. He was discreet and professional, but he didn't play. As soon as he saw the look on Philippe's face he started toward the couple, ready to protect Chastain at all costs.

"Is everything okay, Chastain?" he asked.

"Just fine, James. This is an old friend from my hometown," she answered with a smile as she gently tried to get her arm back from Philippe.

James nodded and strolled away, but he didn't take his eyes off them. Veronica Lewis, the pretty, plump receptionist, went over to James and asked him what was going on. "I have no idea. She says he's an old friend, but he's not looking too friendly to me."

Veronica wrapped one of her natural twists around her finger and looked speculatively at Chastain and Philippe.

"I think you're right," she said in a low voice. "And I think I know why. Look at him and look at those paintings. That's the model in those nudes, James."

His eyes automatically went from the pictures to Philippe and back again. "You may be on to something," he said. "I'd be mad, too, if somebody put me on display like a hunk of meat."

Veronica was too busy looking at Philippe with new eyes to answer him.

Philippe's anger hadn't abated. He wasn't the only one with a temper, though. Chastain was as hot as he was. "I asked you why you were here. Only select invitations were given for tonight's showing," she said nastily.

He hadn't released her arm completely, but instead of clutching her upper arm he'd moved his hand until he was holding hers. With his free hand he reached into his suit coat and pulled out his invitation.

"If you didn't want me here, you shouldn't have sent this," he said in a low voice that nonetheless resonated with fury. "And I can see why you wouldn't want me here to witness *that*." He didn't bother to glance at the three nudes because he knew as well as she did that he was the model she'd painted so exquisitely.

"If you make a spectacle out of this evening you'll live to regret it," she said, barely moving her lips.

"If you don't take those down right now, you'll be the one with regrets. I'll sue you and this gallery and anything else I can think of and it won't be pretty," he vowed.

Anyone else would have cowered under the heated rage and Phillipe's look of pure venom, but Chastain wasn't having it, not tonight. She was about to go off on him but David suddenly appeared with a glass of water.

"Here you are, sweetheart. You've been chatting so much I thought you might be thirsty."

Chastain relaxed at once. "Thank you, David. This is an old friend, Philippe Deveraux. He surprised me tonight. I had no idea he'd be in New York," she said with a slight edge to her voice.

David shook hands with Philippe, which caused him to let go of her hand. "Deveraux? You must be related to Chastain's friend Paris," he said with his usual calm demeanor.

"I'm her brother," Philippe replied. Only Chastain, who knew him way too well, could hear the seething undertone in his voice.

"David, I'm going to chat with Philippe for a few minutes. I haven't talked to Paris in a while and I want to catch up. We'll be right back," she promised as she began to lead Philippe to the elevator. Neither of them spoke until the elevator rose past the gallery, at which point Chastain poked him in the chest with her index finger. "You are a total jackass. I hope you know that."

"And I hope you know you're in a world of trouble, baby girl."

"Arrgh!" Chastain growled as the elevator arrived on the third floor. She walked into the apartment and turned to face him. "You overgrown, arrogant, self-centered jerk! What makes you think I'd invite you to anything, much less my first showing in New York?"

Philippe again took out the invitation and the envelope in which it had come and tossed them at her. "This does."

A sudden barrage of barks came from her bedroom and Chastain turned abruptly to let Lulu out of her crate. Further argument was forestalled as Lulu followed the sound and scent of Philippe into the living room. When Chastain composed herself enough to return she found Philippe sitting on the sofa while Lulu stood in his lap and licked his face fervently.

"I forgot she loves you best," Chastain said.

"That's only because I rescued her," he said between licks.

Chastain looked away from the sentimental reunion and picked up the discarded invitation and its matching envelope. She took one glance at the handwriting and recognized it as Mona's. *I'll deal with her later. Right now I have to deal with this.*

"Look, Philippe, my assistant sent that invitation to you. I knew nothing about it. It wouldn't have occurred to me to invite you because I knew you wouldn't come all the way to New York for me," she began. He cut her off with a sneer.

"It just so happens that I've been in New York for the past two months. I'm working up here."

"You left the law firm?" Chastain blurted out the question without thinking. There were four Deveraux brothers in New Orleans and they practiced law together. Philippe was in environmental law and he was passionate about it.

"No, I didn't leave the firm. I'm on a presidential committee working with the U.N. to push an international initiative for environmental programs. I'll be here another couple of months."

He patted the sofa cushion next to him and Lulu

jumped off his lap and sat obediently. She put one paw on his hand and gave him her happiest smile. Chastain softened when she saw the adorable picture they made, but it didn't last.

"I'm going back downstairs, Chastain. My date is probably wondering where I am. And make sure those pictures come down tonight or you and your friend will find yourselves in the middle of a nasty lawsuit."

He rose to his full six feet five inches and gave Lulu a final pat before leaving. Chastain was left with a crumpled invitation in her clenched fist and the beginnings of a colossal headache. *But if he thinks I'm taking those pictures down he's got another think coming. The days when I did anything to please Philippe Deveraux are over, done and gone.*

Chapter 3

"Well, that was fun. Thanks for bringing me along, Philippe."

A deep growl was his response.

"She seemed really glad to see you," the woman went on. This time her prodding had an effect. Philippe crossed his arms and lowered his thick eyebrows in a fierce glare.

They had left Studio L a few minutes after Philippe returned from talking to Chastain and once they were seated in the limousine that was waiting for them they'd ridden back to her home without a word being spoken. When they'd reached the two-story penthouse she called home, his date finally had enough. She closed the door behind them, locked it and turned to face him with a smile.

"She's even more gorgeous than you said. Would you like a drink?"

"Frederique, if you say another word I'm going to throttle you."

"Don't call me that," she warned. She hated her full name and would only answer to Ricki.

"Then stay out of my business," he replied.

Ricki Fontaine covered a smirk with her hand and repeated her offer of a drink. She was a cousin of the Deverauxes from Lafayette. She had gone to Eastern schools and married a chef who was now a millionaire, thanks to his talent and business savvy. Or maybe he was a billionaire now, Philippe wasn't sure. She was often his favorite cousin but not tonight. Tonight she was a pure pest.

He walked over to the French doors that led out to the terrace and frowned when he couldn't open them. "How do you get out of here?"

"Thinking of jumping, are you? Loverman had everything in here child-proofed. The boys are absolutely fearless as well as being as curious as heck. And the girls are even worse, if that's possible. So, unless your thumbprint can access the keypad over there you won't be flinging yourself off the roof tonight," she said dryly. "Or me, either, because you look mad enough to try it."

"Loverman" was one of her many sappy nicknames for her husband, Antoine. And despite still looking like she was in her twenties, Ricki was the devoted mother of five children under the age of ten. Her long, black hair, smooth dark brown skin and her firm, curvy body all belied her mommy status. Normally Philippe considered her to be quite charming, but she was working his last nerve tonight.

"I'm going to bed, Ricki. Thanks for coming with me," he said in a dead voice.

"Oh, no you're not! You're going to sit down and relax and I'll make you a nice hot drink to loosen your tongue. You have some things to get off your chest. Let me check on my babies and get out of this outfit and I'll be right back," she said.

Philippe groaned as he took off his suit jacket. He had taken off his tie and cuff links and was staring balefully at the twelve-foot Christmas tree that graced the room when Antoine entered the room. He was wearing a silk robe and pajama bottoms, despite the fact that it was only nine o'clock. He put in long hours with his restaurants and usually retired early.

"The baby woke up and Ricki couldn't let her go back to sleep without some mothering." Antoine still had a strong French accent, even though he'd been in America for years. He and Ricki had met when she was in college and it was love at first sight. "She tells me you have some issues to deal with. Let's have a cognac and you can tell me what's putting that look on your face."

Philippe was about to refuse the offer, but somehow the prospect of Antoine's excellent cognac sounded like a plan. Antoine's family owned one of the best vineyards in France and under the management of his brothers they had become one of the biggest importers in the world. Antoine also owned three restaurants in New York and two in New Jersey. His latest project, though, was training homeless and unemployed people in the restaurant business. He said it was his way of giving back to the country that had been so good to him.

They went into the study, which was also a wine cellar. The rich wood that lined the walls held specially made racks that were cleverly disguised behind the paneling and kept each bottle at the perfect temperature. Soon they were each sitting in sinfully comfortable club chairs with a snifter of a hundred-year-old imported cognac that warmed the throat and loosened the tongue.

"So what happened at the showing? Your friend, was she not pleased that you had come?"

Philippe snorted. "*I* wasn't pleased that I had come. I haven't seen Chastain since she dumped me three years ago to take off for France. Chastain and I have been in and out of love since we were kids. I thought at one point that we'd be getting married, but instead she got some genius grant and decided to leave me, leave her family and everything else and work on her painting in Paris," he said with obvious bitterness.

"She'd already been away long enough. She went to college in D.C. and instead of coming home to New Orleans she pranced her little ass off to New York to get an MFA and just stayed here. After Katrina she moved back home and said she was back to stay. But after about four months she got the news that she'd been awarded this big fellowship. That was cool. It really was, because she's extremely talented. She's really gifted, Antoine, I'm not kidding. But the grant didn't have any restrictions on it. She could have done anything she wanted with the money and she chose to just get up and go. She didn't seem to give a damn about what she was leaving behind. She just left." He drained the rest of his snifter and nodded in the affirmative when Antoine offered him a refill.

"I think you mean 'who' she left behind," he said wisely. "You said 'what', but I think you meant to say 'who'."

Philippe shot him a searing look, but gave up and shrugged. "Who meaning me. Yeah, I guess that's what I meant to say. Whatever." Taking another sip, he looked longingly at the expensive humidor on the table.

Antoine understood the look at once and offered Philippe a cigar, which he assured him was excellent. "Better than a Cuban, I promise you. Normally Ricki makes me go out on the terrace, but as long as we air out this room she may let me live."

After lighting the cigars the two men smoked in silence for a moment. Antoine went back to the subject at hand. "So you haven't seen her in three years, you go to her opening and then what? She wasn't glad to see you? She didn't welcome you?"

"She made a fool out of me, that's what she did. She's there looking like she just left a photo shoot and she's got some chump hanging all over her like he owns her. Before I could say anything to her, I happened to look up and see these three huge paintings of a nude man and then I realized they were paintings of me. There I am, big as life, hanging on a wall naked," he snarled. The anger began building again until he felt it might erupt until Antoine interrupted him.

"So? They weren't good pictures, you looked bad, what?"

"Hey, man, come on now. If you walked into an art gallery and saw three nudes, life-size nudes hanging in the middle of the room and you realized it was you, you'd be as mad as I am. That's a total lack of respect. It's like a slap in the face. It's like letting the whole world know that I was just a lay for her. I don't know how she could do something so low-down. But I told her that they're coming down or I'm going to sue her and that gallery for…"

"For what? If someone painted me in the nude I'd be quite flattered, that is if they were beautiful art. Were they caricatures or cartoons? Did you look like an idiot or something?"

"Not really," Philippe admitted. He roughed up his hair with one hand while he thought about the portraits. "It wasn't like my full face was visible."

"And she's very talented, you said? Did she make you look good?"

Philippe was about to answer in the affirmative when he caught himself. "That's really not the point, Antoine. The point is that she painted those pictures without my knowledge or permission and she has them on public display. My privacy has been invaded and she'd going

to remove them from that exhibit or face the conse-
quences."

Ricki sailed into the study wearing pink silk
pajamas and a cashmere robe in the same color.
"You're kidding, right?"

"No, I'm not. Thanks for the talk, Antoine. I'll see
you tomorrow, this time I'm really going to bed."

He left the room, leaving the couple alone.

"Loverman, what did we say about cigars?" Ricki
waved her hand in front of her face with a grimace.

"Sorry, darling. Philippe looked like he could use
one. I've never seen him this upset about anything
before."

Ricki got comfortable on her husband's lap, snug-
gling next to his heart with a contented sigh. "Philippe
is actually one of my more mild-mannered cousins.
They all have hot tempers, but Philippe was always the
most laid-back of the bunch. He must have really been
crazy in love to react like that."

Antoine stroked her silky hair and inhaled the fragrance that always clung to it. "How bad were the portraits? He seems to think they were a source of
humiliation."

Ricki turned her head so she could kiss his neck. "To
tell you the truth, I didn't really get to see them that well.
I noticed them, but I was busy looking at these exquisite
renderings of Bricktop and Richard Wright. This lady
has an amazing gift, Antoine. I was staring at the paintings and the next thing I knew Philippe was dragging me
out of there like the place was about to explode.

"But I want some of her work," she said thoughtfully. "As soon as I take the children to school tomorrow the baby and I are going to have a little field trip. And I'm going to find out what's going on with Philippe. I think I should call his sister to get the real scoop." She was reaching for the phone when he stopped her.

"Call her tomorrow. Your husband is also crazy in love and he wants to show you how much."

Ricki dissolved in sexy giggles, which were quickly drowned by her Loverman's lips.

Philippe stood in the shower and let the hot water beat down over his body as though it could wash away the strange feelings that were roiling around inside. He'd always prided himself on being the man in control, the calm in the storm. Hell, he'd had to be the mediator in so many of his brother's fights that he'd learned to control his emotions and keep a clear head. And all it took was one look at Chastain for all of his mature powers of reason to desert him. He'd done much worse than dive off the deep end, so to speak. He'd plunged into the shallow end of the pool of stupid and hit his head.

He finally turned off the water and stepped out of the huge circular shower enclosed in glass. He used one of Ricki's thick towels to dry off and went into the bedroom to find something to sleep in. He normally slept nude, but he tried to exercise some modesty since he was in a home with small children. He'd already found out that they would occasionally burst into the room to say hello without an invitation. He put on a pair of boxers and an old T-shirt and sat on the side of the bed.

Chastain had always been a pretty girl, but during the time she'd been in France she had turned into a beauty. It wasn't just the fact that he hadn't seen her in three years. There was something remarkable in her transformation. When he'd spotted her across the room at Studio L, it was like all the air had been sucked out of his lungs. The dress she was wearing looked like it was made for her alone. It fit her like a second skin. It looked like a second skin, too, because it was so close to the honey color of her perfect complexion. Her hair was still short and ultra-stylish, showing off her beautiful eyes, deep dimples and the perfect lips that could kiss like no one else in the world, as he well knew.

He remembered the first time he'd ever laid eyes on Chastain, the day she'd come home with his sister, Paris. The family had recently moved to New Orleans and Paris was going to a Catholic school for girls. She hadn't been looking forward to a new school but meeting her new friend Chastain had made her day. She'd promptly brought her home to meet the family and Philippe could remember it as if it was yesterday. She was a little thing with bony legs, a bandage on her knee and long, brown braids. One of her kneesocks was up and the other one was down around her ankle and her blouse was halfway tucked into her plaid uniform skirt. Instead of having her navy blue blazer on as it should have been, hers was tied around her waist and she was wearing big round eyeglasses with a piece of tape on the frame front. For some reason she was the cutest thing he'd ever seen and his opinion had never changed.

Even now, after she'd stepped on his heart twice and exposed his naked body to the world, he still couldn't bring himself to despise her. After all they'd been through, all she'd put him through, something about her still called to him like a siren. But that didn't mean he was going to let her off the hook. If those pictures stayed up, they were going to court.

Chapter 4

At Studio L, Chastain's mood was no better than Philippe's. After all the guests had left, she went up to the loft, accompanied by David. Mona wisely decided to stay downstairs for a moment, ostensibly to see to the guest book that all the attendees had signed, but she didn't escape a dark look from Chastain that meant a conversation was inevitable at a later time. David asked if she wanted something to drink and she nodded.

"Just let me get Lulu out of her crate. She likes to be in there while I'm away, but she insists on being out the instant I return." In a few minutes, she was back, taking a seat at the bar that separated the well-appointed kitchen from the dining area. Lulu was seeking

David's attention while he poured two cups of steaming tea that smelled delicious.

While Chastain sipped hers, he played with Lulu and fondled her ears. "So what happened tonight? I could see that Philippe upset you in some way. What was he saying to you?"

"Nothing much. He just said that if I didn't take down the nudes he would sue you and me. He seemed to think that he was the model and that I was invading his privacy," she said. She didn't look at him while she was speaking. She was busy running her index finger around the top of the cup.

"He said what?" David looked incredulous before reaching over to take her free hand. "He can't sue us. He doesn't have any basis for a lawsuit, regardless of the subject of the paintings. It wouldn't even get to court."

Chastain allowed him to rub her hand and wrist and enjoyed the comforting sensation. "I don't know about that. The law is something he knows very well. He's a lawyer, his three brothers are lawyers, his late mother was a lawyer and his father is a state Supreme Court justice. He doesn't play when it comes to the law."

"Maybe not, but I think tonight was more about love than law. He did model for those paintings, didn't he?"

Chastain jumped and pulled her hand away. "No! Well, not exactly. We did have a relationship a long time ago. And yes, when I painted the pictures I was thinking about Philippe, but it wasn't like he was sitting in the room. I painted them from memory," she said with a slight defensive edge to her voice.

"He must have meant a great deal to you," David said quietly.

Chastain met his eyes for the first time and flushed under his steady gaze. His beautiful eyes were warm with concern and locked on hers. She had to answer him honestly; there was no point in lying. "At one time, he meant more to me than anything else. But that was a long time ago."

"Before graduate school?" he probed gently.

"Before I started college, actually," she told him. "He broke my little teenage heart a few days before Christmas when I was a senior in high school."

David leaned over and kissed her forehead. "It was his loss," he said.

"And then he broke it again before I went to Europe," she said slowly, watching David's face for his reaction.

"I see. So he blew two opportunities to be with you," he said. "He's a bigger fool than I would have imagined. Come walk me to the door. You need to get some sleep because you're going to be hella busy for the next few weeks. The showing is going to be the talk of the town, Chastain."

"You're right. If we get sued by the Deveraux family, everybody on the East Coast is going to know about it," she said wryly.

"He's not stupid, Chastain. He might be jealous and cranky because he can see that he threw away two chances of a lifetime with you, but he's not crazy enough to try to pursue a frivolous lawsuit like that. It'll all blow over, believe me."

"I wish I could."

"You can."

He held out his hands and she took them, rising from the tall stool. She and Lulu walked him to the door and she wasn't surprised when he kissed her. He did it slowly and gently and it was warm and reassuring, like everything about David.

"See you tomorrow, Chastain. I'll send Mona up. I have a feeling she's hiding from you."

"And you know this. Tell her I'm up here with a blunt instrument just for her head."

"You're crazy. Sleep well."

"Mona, I'm not going to kill you, at least not in front of Lulu. She's much too delicate to witness murder, aren't you, sweetie?"

Lulu was making growling noises as she burrowed under the many pillows at the head of Chastain's bed. Her head popped up as Chastain spoke and both women laughed at her disheveled look. "Shake it out, Lulu, you got crazy face," Chastain said. The little dog shook her head vigorously, restoring her usual appearance. "Now as for you, Miss Mona, I don't know what to say to you. When had you planned on telling me you sent that invitation?"

Both women were wearing pajamas and Chastain was applying cream to her face as she spoke. Chastain was in the middle of the bed and Mona was perched on a broad hardwood bench with a thick upholstered cushion.

"I wasn't trying to start anything, I really wasn't. It's just that I was trying to invite everyone who was close to you. I just went down your address book." Her face was pink from embarrassment. "Besides, I know how close you are to his sister and the rest of the family, so I thought it would be strange if you didn't invite him, too. And, I um, I um…"

Chastain stopped smoothing the cream onto her neck. "*Um,* what? Go ahead and spit it out, the worst has already happened. You *um* what?"

Mona bit her lip in an effort to look innocent. "Okay, well, you talked about Philippe so much and I could tell, well, I always felt like he was your true soul mate and I thought if you two got together in New York at Christmastime anything could happen," she said hurriedly.

Chastain didn't lash out at her, although she did try to sic Lulu on her. "Go bite her, little girl. Bite her big toe," she urged.

"I'm not going to say you were wrong in what you did, but your reasoning was way off base. The Philippe Deveraux ship has sailed, as you could see for yourself tonight. Did you happen to notice the woman he was with? His date? That's the kind of woman he really goes for, tall, dark, curvy and delicious. He and his brothers all have a thing for a woman they can hang on to. But she's got to be beautiful and brilliant, too. All of their women are the business, honey."

"So? You're the business, too, Chastain. Nobody can say you're not," Mona said indignantly.

Chastain finished applying the moisturizing cream and rubbed the rest of it into her hands, which Lulu tried to lick. "Stop it! This is some expensive stuff," she chided her. "It's not just that, Mona. New Orleans is very class-conscious. If you're not from the right family and you don't belong to the right circles, you just don't fit in."

Mona made a face. "Excuse me, I'm from D.C. and my father's a diplomat, remember? I know more about snobs than you ever care to hear, trust me. Please tell me that's not what broke you up. You're a successful artist, Chastain. How could you not fit in anywhere you choose?"

"You're talking about Chastain version 2009. You didn't know me when I was a scrawny little tomboy running the streets of the Quarter like a foster child," Chastain said. "There's a lifetime of difference from then to now."

Mona laughed. "Are you trying to tell me *you* were a 'hood rat? Because I'm not going to believe you, it's not possible. You always look like a page out of *Vogue,* for heaven's sake."

"I was more of a 'hood *mouse,* I guess. I cleaned up well, I'll grant you that. But back in the day I was a mouthy, mean little brat who sold fake voodoo dolls and bogus love potions in my Uncle Toto's shop. If I hadn't gotten a scholarship to a Catholic school I might have ended up behind bars by now," she said, laughing at the expression on Mona's face.

"So how did you and Philippe get together? Don't

tell me you didn't because now that I know who the model is for those nudes, I know there had to something going on between you two."

"You're an inquisitive little thing, aren't you? I got to be friends with Paris, Philippe's sister. She's the only girl in a family of five boys and she was quite the tomboy, too. So we kind of latched on to each other. My mother died when I was a baby and hers died when she was really young so we had that in common. We were best friends, still are, as a matter of fact. I was in her wedding and when she had her first baby, a little girl, I was the godmother. She's pregnant again, this time with twins," Chastain said with a smile.

"Don't change the subject. You and Philippe, how, when and where?"

"Paris and I were like sisters and that meant that I was like a member of the family. Her brothers picked on me and I fought back. Philippe finally stopped picking on me the summer before my senior year of high school. Paris was in Atlanta for the summer with her aunt Lillian and her cousins, and I was working in my grandmother's restaurant, Mama T's. I was gawky and skinny and I still had a mouth on me. But I'd gotten rid of the braids and the glasses and I was wearing a little makeup. It got me better tips.

"Anyway, Philippe was working that summer and he used to come in for lunch almost every day. He always sat in my section and when he wasn't with his brothers he would act like a real gentleman. We didn't snap on each other and play the dozens. We just had nice conversations. Then we started going for walks and going to the movies and stuff and it was really nice. When he kissed me for the first time it felt like he really meant it," she said softly. "It was my first real kiss. Well, the first one that didn't end with me punching the daylights out of the guy. I didn't play back then. Still don't."

"And then?"

Chastain closed her eyes. "I don't know why I'm telling you all this. This is why I'm glad I'm an only child. There was nobody to get all up in my business," she muttered.

Relenting, she continued the story. "We started seeing each other, but we kept it on the down low because we wanted to keep it private. It seemed much more special that way. And besides, my grandmother Tippy didn't like him too much. It wasn't him in particular. It was rich boys in general she had a problem with, I think. She knew I had feelings for Philippe and she did everything in her power to discourage me, which of course made me even more determined. She used to say, 'He's all wrong for you, *cher.* No good gon' come of this. You from the Quarter and he from the Row and no need to think that you can make a match wid him.'

"So we were like the bayou Romeo and Juliet. It was so romantic and sweet, at least I thought it was. Of course we made love and it was wonderful. I wasn't expecting that much, but when you're young and uninhibited, first-time sex can be as good as first love. We kept it up until the Christmas of my senior year. He told me that when I went to college I shouldn't wait for him, that I should feel free to see anyone I wanted. Well, I wasn't stupid. I knew that meant that he was tired of me and he was kicking me to the curb."

"But maybe that wasn't what he meant," Mona protested. "He was, what, a year older than you? Teenage boys aren't that sophisticated, Chastain."

Chastain shot her a sideward look and asked, "Have you ever told someone that you should see other people?"

"Yes, once or twice."

"And what did you mean by that?"

"Lose my number, I'm bored with you," Mona admitted.

"Exactly. I was dying inside but I didn't shed a tear. I told him sure, fine, and then I made sure I got a full scholarship to someplace far away from Louisiana. I very rarely spoke to him after that. Even after we broke up, we kept it on the down low because I didn't want to ruin my friendship with Paris. It was all good in the end because after I finished my bachelor's degree I came to New York and got my master's and I liked it up here so much I just stayed. If it hadn't been for what my uncle calls 'that mean bitch Katrina', I would've continued to live here quite happily."

"But you had good reasons to go back to New Orleans after the storm. It only made sense," Mona said.

"Yeah, it did. But what didn't make sense was me getting involved with Philippe again. As soon as I was back in the same area code as him, I was back in his arms like the big dummy I am."

Mona's eyes got huge. "Dare I ask what happened then?"

"This is what I missed by not having a younger sister, isn't it? Thank you, Jesus, for sparing me," Chastain said, staring at the ceiling. "He dumped me again, Mona. On Christmas Eve."

Mona covered her face with her hands and let out a little shriek.

Chastain chuckled grimly. "I've been wondering what it would take to shut you up."

Chapter 5

September 2005
New Orleans, Ninth Ward

Chastain stood on what used to be a sidewalk and choked down her own tears. It was like some prehistoric beast had ravaged the city. Houses were destroyed, trees were turned over and the streets were littered with broken limbs and exposed roots. Debris was still floating everywhere and the sight was horrible. Furniture, shoes, cars, a child's bicycle and other bits and pieces of people's lives churned in the filthy water. Chastain tried to take in the enormity of what she was seeing, but she couldn't. It was just too much to process. She covered her mouth with one hand and the tears rolled faster and harder.

A touch on her shoulder made her turn around, but she wasn't afraid. As soon as she felt his big hand, she knew it was Philippe. She felt the same soft thrill that always coursed through her body whenever he was near her. He turned her around to face him and wrapped his long arms around her.

"You shouldn't be out here by yourself."

"How did you know where I was?"

"I know you, Cerise," he said as his arms tightened. Cerise, the French word for cherry, was his special nickname for her.

"It's so awful, Philippe. It's worse than I imagined," she said sobbing.

"I know it is, baby. You can't keep standing out here in this mess. Come on, let's go."

He kissed her forehead, her weeping eyes and her cheeks, and warmth flooded her body. She went with him willingly and in a relatively short time they were at his house. He opened the door and she went in first. Once inside the foyer, they looked into each other's eyes deeply and intently. In one movement they were in each other's arms, kissing like this was the only moment they would ever have together.

Philippe's lips covered Chastain's and his tongue plundered their sweetness as she opened herself to him. He put his hands under her behind and lifted her so her legs could wrap around his waist. Their mouths were fused together, tongues stroking, temperatures rising as he walked to the stairs that would take them to his bedroom. As soon as they reached the bed they were tearing at each other's clothes with an urgent need to join their bodies. Philippe's jeans and briefs were finally discarded in one direction while her blouse went the other way, followed by her bra. He didn't bother to take off her lace-trimmed thong panties. He moved them aside with a long finger, feeling the moisture that had already pooled between her thighs.

His rock-hard penis slid into her with fierce precision, a hard thrust that was followed by more. Their hips were rocking back and forth and their mutual need was answered by a shattering climax that shook them both at the same time. Still locked together, they gradually slowed down long enough to remove the rest of their clothing so that there was nothing to separate them. The familiar feel of his silky-rough chest hair against her breasts made her want more of him, as much as he could give her. His mouth was driving her crazy, biting her neck softly between lingering kisses.

When he licked her between her breasts and began sucking her hardened, ultra-sensitized nipples, she tightened her walls on his manhood and pumped until she was on the verge of another climax. Philippe rolled onto his back and held her hips as she pumped harder and faster. His upward thrusts matched hers until a second, more intense orgasm shook their bodies wet with the sweet, steamy sweat of release.

Maybe it was because they were so emotionally charged from the aftermath of the storm, or maybe it was because they'd realized how much they cared about each other, but whatever the reason, they continued to make love until they couldn't move a single limb. They fell deeply asleep in each other's arms and stayed that way until morning.

December 2, 2009
New York

Chastain couldn't believe how much she'd revealed to Mona before going to bed. There were certain things that she left out, like the details of her sex life with Philippe, but she'd given the young woman an earful. On the one hand, talking about her sad little love life was kind of cathartic. It helped put her strange encounter with him into perspective. Mona had to get the last word in, though. When she was getting ready to go to her bedroom she said something that got Chastain thinking.

"I had forgotten about that stupid invitation until Philippe showed up last night. When I saw you and David together I thought that's the kind of man you need to be with. I'd pay somebody to look at me the way he looks at you. I really would."

Chastain went to bed with David on her mind, but he didn't stay there long. All night long she dreamed about Philippe, about that day in New Orleans and how they made love for hours without uttering a word. Their bodies and their souls had done all the communicating. It was much later when Philippe had said, "I love you." The dream was so vivid that she woke up expecting him to be there with her, but there was only Lulu, curled into a tight ball with one bright eye open.

"You slept just fine, didn't you? I was the one tossing and turning all night with X-rated memories. I'm going to take a shower and get dressed and then we'll go for a long walk. How does that sound?"

Lulu's answered her with a big yawn.

When Mona got up about thirty minutes later, Chastain was dressed and ready to go. She looked fierce in a pair of black trousers, an ivory cowl-necked cashmere sweater topped with a red belt and black boots. Lulu was also dressed in her snappy red coat with black velvet buttons.

"Good morning, sweetie. There's coffee and I made beignets. I'm taking girlfriend for a walk."

Mona rubbed her sleepy eyes. "My God, how can you be so perky at this hour? You went to bed the same time I did and I feel like fresh hell," she moaned.

"It's because I'm pure of heart," Chastain said with a laugh. "Pull yourself together and I'll see you in a half hour or so."

James and Veronica were already in the gallery when she went downstairs. They chatted for a few minutes and then Chastain and Lulu set off down Lexington Avenue. The cold air was refreshing and for once the barrage of holiday decorations and the constant reminders of Christmas didn't bother her. She felt really good, as a matter of fact. She felt as if she was better able to deal with whatever Philippe chose to dish out. "If he wants to be a jackass, then I've got something for him. I don't know what it is, exactly, but my grandma didn't raise a fool. I'll take his head off and hand it to him, won't I, little girl?"

Lulu was trotting along beside her drawing all kinds of attention in her little coat. She loved being outside and she especially loved meeting new people. The two of them looked like a Macy's ad. Chastain's coat was a black-and-white hound's-tooth swing coat and she had on a red beret and scarf that picked up the colors in Lulu's coat. Chastain was used to hearing compliments on her fancy little dog, so when they were returning to Studio L and she heard a little girl in a stroller squeal, "Doggie," it was par for the course.

She was keeping a careful eye on Lulu because she was very fond of babies and she'd try to kiss them. They stopped for a red light and as luck would have it, so did the stroller. "Doggie!" Lulu reacted at once, going over to the carriage to meet its occupant. Chastain spoke to Lulu in French, telling her to sit down and be a lady. The child's mother wasn't alarmed in the least, however.

"Demetria loves dogs," she confided. "She's not afraid of them at all. Allow me to introduce myself. I'm Ricki Fontaine. I was at your showing last night, but I didn't get to meet you," she said charmingly.

Chastain's eyes left Lulu and her hand tightened on the lead. She stared into the sparkling brown eyes of the beautiful woman who'd been Philippe's date. She felt a little faint, especially after she took a good look at the dimpled little girl in the stroller. That child was a Deveraux—there was no denying it. Was this what Philippe had been up to since she went to Europe?

Philippe awoke with the alacrity of a dead man about to walk. He'd had a rough night. Dreams of Chastain had started almost the moment he closed his eyes. It was as if his subconscious had deliberately picked the most profoundly sensual dream possible, the one about their reunion in New Orleans after Katrina. He'd heard she was back, but he hadn't seen her. He went out looking for her and knew instinctively where she would be. When he found her forlorn figure he took her in his arms and couldn't let her go. They had gone back to his house and made love for hours. It was some of the best lovemaking he'd ever had. Nothing had compared to it since and he knew nothing ever would.

He was the one who'd introduced Chastain into the art of making love. She was an apt and eager pupil, surprisingly uninhibited and natural. She had taught him as much as he taught her, not from experience but from her heart. He could never forget that he was her first lover. She understood at once when he started calling her Cerise. It was because he treasured her gift to him above all else. And she would probably never speak to him again after the way he'd behaved last night. A cold shower seemed his just reward for his colossal stupidity.

After he had showered, shaved and dressed, he joined Antoine in the kitchen. The housekeeper was there, but Antoine was doing the cooking. He always made breakfast for his family and he insisted on doing the same for Philippe. "A cup of coffee isn't going to give you the energy you need for the day. A good meal and a good woman are what you need. I can make you a delicious omelet, but the woman, that's up to you," he said with a rakish grin.

Philippe decided to let that one pass. He'd had a long dream about the perfect woman, but he wasn't about to share that information with Antoine, no matter how much he liked the guy. "It's quiet in here," he observed.

Antoine agreed. "Yes, it's like a tomb here without my little angels. Ricki took them to school. She refuses to leave it to the driver. She says it's her responsibility and her pleasure." He took another sip of the espresso he'd prepared and looked over at Philippe, who was checking his BlackBerry.

"You seem to be in a better mood today," he observed.

"I think I am," Philippe replied. "I owe you for listening to me vent. You may have prevented me from making a grave mistake."

Antoine looked pleased. "So you've decided to let it go? No lawsuit?"

"I don't think it's going to come to that. I have something else in mind. A mutually satisfactory compromise is what I have planned."

"An excellent idea. I'm sure your friend will agree to it. It's a good solution."

Philippe chuckled. "She may not be thrilled about

it, but she'll listen to reason. Once I make her an offer she can't refuse, she'll see things my way."

Antoine laughed in return. "You sound like the God-father. Should I kiss your ring?"

"I'd actually prefer it if you didn't put your lips anywhere near me, thanks." Philippe shuddered as Antoine laughed while he whisked the omelet.

Chapter 6

Chastain was pleased that she didn't pass out when the woman introduced herself. She drew on the yoga classes she'd been taking since she was in college and found the calming inner strength to smile at her. "I'm Chastain Thibodaux. So nice to meet you," she murmured. She even held the door to Studio L open to accommodate Demetria's stroller. Lulu was happy to see that her new best friend was coming with them. She barked her happy bark and stood on her hind legs to give the baby a kiss.

"Lulu, no! Sit, Lulu," she said firmly. "I apologize for my dog, but she loves men, babies, children, other dogs, cats and all forms of life. She's very friendly."

Ricki didn't seem to mind Lulu's attention. "I've been thinking about getting a dog for my children. I was just waiting for Demetria to be potty trained," she said. "I have five children and my husband and I can't potty train a puppy and a child at the same time. There's only so much we can handle," she said with a smile.

Chastain's ears were buzzing with that bit of information. Philippe was having an affair with a married woman? That was impossible.

Ricki didn't notice the blank look on Chastain's face, she just kept on talking. "I was here last night with my cousin, Philippe Deveraux, but I didn't get to see everything. You're so talented that I had to come back. I hope it's okay that I brought Demetria. She's very well behaved but I'm not letting her out of the stroller. She has moves like Jackie Joyner-Kersee. I can't keep up with her."

His cousin. Well that explained the resemblance. The baby looked like a Deveraux because her mother was a Deveraux. *She must be one of the cousins from Lafayette,* Chastain thought.

"Ricki, I'll be happy to give you a personal tour if you let me take Miss Lulu upstairs and get her situated."

Mona appeared out of nowhere and said she would do it. "Give me your coats and I'll take them, too. Chastain, you've had quite a few calls this morning, I put them all on your desk," she added.

"Thanks, Mona. Mona Morgan, this is Ricki Fontaine. She was here last night with her cousin Philippe and she came back today to get a better look."

"I'm not just looking. I brought my checkbook," Ricki said. "I really liked what I saw last night."

Mona took Lulu and the coats away and the two women started walking through the gallery. The works were divided into categories. Drawings, charcoal and pastels, acrylics and oils were grouped together. There were some collages as well as some boxes that were like cross-sections of houses. Ricki was thoroughly impressed.

"You're beyond talented, Chastain. You are gifted. Did you always want to be an artist?"

"More or less. I was always painting, drawing, making dolls or hair ornaments or something. I did contemplate being an exotic dancer for a while, but my grandmother assured me she'd hang me from a pole before she let me dance on one."

Ricki laughed. "You're kidding, aren't you?"

"My great uncle has a show bar in N'awlins. The thought crossed my mind a few times. I also wanted to tend bar at my other uncle's juke joint, but that was vetoed, too. My grandmother was quite relieved when I decided to study art."

They took a real liking to each other while they walked. Chastain found Ricki to be down-to-earth and very friendly and her little girl was a real charmer. She kept looking around saying "Doggie?" and "Mama, where is *la petite chienne?*"

Chastain looked surprised until Ricki explained that her children were all bilingual. "My husband is French and they've been speaking both languages since they could talk."

"*Chienne,* Mama?" Demetria was still looking for Lulu.

"That settles it. I'm going to have to get a dog for

my babies. Maybe two of them. You should come over for dinner and bring Lulu. The children would love it and I'd love to introduce you to my husband."

Chastain was about to accept when Ricki said that Philippe was living with them while he was working in the city.

"Thank you so much, but that might not be such a good idea. Philippe and I aren't on good terms right now," she said frankly.

"Then he'll have to get over it, won't he? You can ask my husband, Chastain, the word 'no' isn't in my vocabulary. Ask Paris, she'll tell you the same thing. Philippe may have his undies in a bunch over those gorgeous nudes, but he has no reason to. They're amazing, like everything here. I'm going to keep asking you until you give in, so get ready," she warned with a smile.

Demetria was getting tired, so Ricki prepared to leave. True to her word, she bought two large oils and a smaller pastel. They would remain on display until the end of the show but it was lovely to be able to put a sold tag on the pieces.

"And I will be calling you often until you agree to come over. You're not just Philippe's friend, you're a friend of the family and you're welcome anytime," she insisted.

As she was leaving, David was coming in and Chastain was delighted to show him the huge check Ricki had just written. "You know what? I think I'm a real artist," she gloated.

"Sweetheart, haven't you been listening to me? I've

been telling you that for years. How about I take you out to celebrate?"

"I'd love it. And it's my treat," she added, waving the check.

"Never. If I take you out, I pay," he said firmly.

Chastain got a little chill when he said that because his declaration sounded so much like something Philippe would say. She shook it off and assured him that she wouldn't arm-wrestle him for the bill. "What time should I be ready?"

"I'll pick you up at eight." He leaned over and pressed a sweet kiss on her cheek.

It was barely six when Philippe reached Studio L, but it was dark and a fine snow was falling. He entered the gallery and took off his black overcoat. Putting it over his arm, he began to look at Chastain's work. In a few minutes he was lost in the worlds she'd created. Her use of color, the way she arranged her subjects, the way she rendered them. All of those elements combined to make her a brilliant artist. He was examining a triptych that depicted a night at Bricktop's, the legendary jazz club that bore the owner's nickname, when a familiar fragrance wafted to his nose.

"Chastain, these are spectacular. I can hear the music when I look at this," he said.

"How did you know I was here? I thought I was being quiet," she replied.

"I smelled you. You're the only woman I know who

wears Magie Noire and you're the only one who should."

He looked down at her and saw the consternation on her face. "Are you trying to butter me up before you hit me with a subpoena?"

"No, I'm trying to tell you how much I admire your work. I feel like I'm right there in the nightclub." He turned back to the three-paneled painting and added, "I'm sure Ada 'Bricktop' Smith is smiling about this right now."

"That's why I went to France. I wanted to explore the place where people like James Baldwin, Richard Wright and Bricktop lived, people who had to leave America in order to live with freedom and dignity. I wanted to portray their experiences to the world."

"You did it," he affirmed quietly. "I didn't think it was possible for you to get better, but you did. What I'm seeing here almost made it worth it to lose you." He looked down into her eyes, the eyes that could always see right into his heart. "Almost."

Chastain's right hand went to her earlobe and she fingered her earring, a sure sign of emotional vulnerability. Her face softened and just as quickly her expression turned cold as she crossed her arms tightly over her enticing breasts.

"Why are you here, Philippe? Are you looking for more evidence to sue me or something?"

"Can we talk for a minute? I think we can work this out to our mutual satisfaction if we can have a conversation," he said.

She gave him a skeptical look, but agreed. "Come upstairs with me. I have to feed Her Highness," she said, but she didn't uncross her arms.

Lulu raced around the loft in gleeful circles after she eagerly greeted Philippe. Chastain put her food dish down and put fresh water in her bowl with two ice cubes, the way she liked it. She came into the living area and sat down on a big ottoman a safe distance away from the sofa where Philippe was sitting.

"Okay, here we are. What did you want to talk about?"

"How have you been?"

Chastain looked stunned by the question. "What do you care? I haven't seen you in three years, haven't heard a word from you, then you come bursting in here on the biggest night of my life threatening me and now you ask me how I've been? Is this some kind of ploy to get me to admit something?"

"I deserve that, Chastain, but no, it's not. You're right. I did come here yesterday like I was conducting a police raid and I apologize. And I haven't seen you for three years and I didn't have the decency to say hello, to ask how you'd been or congratulate you on your show. I'm trying to behave like a civilized human being and I really want to know how you are, how you liked Europe and all that. Isn't that how old friends behave?"

Chastain's face was still wary. "Is that what we are now, old friends? I hardly recognize you, Philippe. I should be asking you how *you* are. What's with the short hair and the fancy suits? What happened to the jeans and sneakers and radical T-shirts? What have you been up to since I've been gone?"

Lulu had been drinking water noisily in the kitchen and came bounding out with a wet chin. Chastain used her hand to wipe off the water while Philippe watched her closely.

"I got the chance to do some important work with various government agencies and I didn't want to scare them off by looking like a Greenpeace reject. I also did a lot of campaign work for Barack Obama during the election and I wanted to look more professional. You don't approve?"

"Me? I'm not in a position to approve or disapprove of anything you do. If you like it, I love it," she said nonchalantly. "As far as your initial question, the answer is I've been well, I enjoyed Europe, I went to London, Milan and a few other places, I acquired certain artistic skills and techniques and I made a lot of friends," she recited.

"Friends like that David?"

"It's none of your business," she said pointedly. "But since you're nosy enough to ask, David and I have been friends for years. I've known him since graduate school."

"Friends or lovers?" His voice was as indifferent as if he was inquiring about the weather. That seemed to light a fuse under Chastain.

"Philippe, what do you want? You said you wanted

to talk to me about something that would be mutually agreeable and that topic in no way includes my sex life," she said with a slightly curled lip.

"So you do have a sex life," he drawled.

"That's it," she said hotly. She pointed to the elevator door. "I'm not playing any mind games with you, so you can just leave. And by the way, if you have any more problems with my nude paintings you can refer them to my lawyer. As you saw they are still on display and they will continue to be as long as I'm showing at Studio L or any other place I want to exhibit them. You got that, buddy?"

"That's the real reason I'm here," he answered. "I want to buy all three of them."

His words were slightly muffled by Lulu's happy growls as she attacked a toy she'd found under a chair, but Chastain heard him very clearly.

"You pompous ass, they're not for sale! Was *this* your big idea? You thought you'd walk in here smooth-talking and looking good and I'd just fold when you waved your wallet at me? Bite me, Philippe. If you think I'm going to sell you those paintings so you can destroy them to satisfy your ego you're a bigger jerk than I thought you were and that hardly seems possible. Get out of here before I call the cops to drag you out."

She had stood up and was pointing toward the doorway again with one hand on her hip and menace in her eyes. She was hot and if he didn't leave she would probably hurl something at him, but it didn't stop him from wanting her. He'd always loved her hot-headed disposition and it seemed as though her time abroad hadn't diminished it one bit.

"Chastain, I'm not going to destroy the paintings and I'm not going to sue you. It would bring more attention to me than to you. I'm not even going to try to explain how I feel about them anymore. But I have one question for you. If you can answer it, I'll leave and never darken your door again, if that's what you want."

Her arm dropped to her side, although she kept a hand on her hip. "What?"

"Why did you paint them?"

Chastain's face flushed to a deep bronze and she couldn't utter a sound. Philippe leaned back into the sofa cushions with a satisfied expression. Things were getting really interesting in the loft. He couldn't wait to hear what she had to say.

Chapter 7

"I'm sorry, I didn't know you had company," Mona apologized. She'd stepped off the elevator and looked shocked to see Philippe in the middle of a love fest with Lulu.

Chastain had never been happier to see anyone in her life. "That's okay, sweetie. Philippe was just leaving, weren't you?"

He had stretched out his long legs and one of his arms was spread across the back of the sofa. He didn't look like he was in any hurry to move. The look on his face was ridiculously smug. Lulu was sprawled across his lap and it was all too much for Chastain.

"Mona, I don't believe we've met formally," he said with the legendary Deveraux charm. He eased Lulu off his lap and stood up, walking toward Mona with his hand outstretched. "I'm Philippe Deveraux."

"I, um, yes you are," Mona murmured. "It's nice to meet you. Would you care for a cocktail, wine, coffee, anything?"

"Yes, I would," he answered.

"No, he wouldn't," Chastain said firmly. "I have a date and I need to change. Philippe, we'll have to talk some other time. Let me get your coat," she added hurriedly.

"Here's your coat."

"What's your hurry? Is that how we're doing this?" Philippe looked and sounded amused, adding to Chastain's annoyance.

"Yep, that's how it's going down. I'll see you when I see you. Goodbye."

"I'll call you tomorrow," he said.

"You don't have my number."

"That's the one thing I do have," he said with a damnably sexy smile.

Chastain huffed as she practically dragged him across the room to the elevator. "Philippe, I'm not in the mood for this. Goodbye," she repeated impatiently.

"I'll have to put you in a better mood tomorrow. Because we are going to talk and you will give me an answer to my question. Have a good evening." Before she could stop him he kissed his forefinger, pressed it on her cheek and departed.

Mona was still looking dazed as the elevator descended to the main floor. "You didn't have to kick him out the door, Chastain. That was kind of rude, wasn't it?"

"It was self-preservation, Mona. Look at you. All he did was shake your hand and you look Deverauxed."

"I look what?"

Chastain started toward her bedroom. "You look Deverauxed, Monie. That's the effect those darned men have on women. All you have to do is get within five feet of one of them and you get all mushy and goo goo-eyed. I thought you were made of tougher stuff than that, girlfriend."

"But I didn't get a real good look at him before. Those eyes and those cheekbones and that deep voice," Mona said as she followed Chastain. "He has beautiful hands, did you ever notice that?"

Chastain was undressing in front of the open closet and looking for an appropriate outfit to wear. "Mona, those hands have touched every inch of my body in ways I can't discuss with you. So yes, I have had occasion to notice them."

"Wow. Are there any more of them at home? I could use a man like that for my personal edification," Mona said as she helped Chastain find a dress to wear.

"Oh, that'll work. Can you hand me that citron-colored dress, the knit one? Thanks, Monie."

"But what about Philippe? Does he have any brothers?"

"Yes and they all look alike. They're all tall, fair-skinned with that wavy black hair and the piercing eyes. He even has a twin brother named Lucien, but he's married. He and Nicole have a little girl and they're expecting another baby in a couple of months.

Julian is married, too. Wade is still single, or at least he was last I heard."

She turned around so Mona could zip her up. The dress was another vintage number with long sleeves and a deep scoop neck. It was close fitting with a tight skirt that fell to just below the knee. She wore a thin bronze belt with it and was putting on some very chic knee-high boots when Mona asked if she had a picture of Wade.

"Don't go there, Monie. If you want to see what he looks like, look at Philippe if you ever see him again. Personally, I don't plan on seeing him. I plan to stay as far away from him as possible," she mumbled.

"So you say. He's going to call you tomorrow so you can answer his question. What's the question and why couldn't you give him an answer tonight?"

Chastain was putting on gold bangle bracelets to match the small thick gold hoops in her ears. "Let's just say it was a question I had no intention of answering, which is why I was so thrilled that you came upstairs when you did. My days of confiding in that man are over. I bared my heart and soul to Philippe once upon a time and I have no intentions of backtracking. Let sleeping dogs lie, or whatever."

"So there's no way you'd get back with Philippe? Not ever?"

"Never ever," Chastain said as she went to brush her teeth. She put a large towel on like a bib and leaned over the glass bowl sink.

"A couple of days ago you thought I had the big

pants for David and now you're trying to throw me at Philippe. What is your problem, Mona? Are you turning into a panderer or something?"

She brushed her teeth quickly but thoroughly and followed by rinsing with organic mouthwash. Mona was playing with Lulu on the bed when she came out of the bathroom.

"You're the one that said you and David were friends," she reminded Chastain. "Friendship is wonderful, but romance is the real prize and it seems to me that one or both of those men would make a fine romance for you. That's all I'm saying."

"Do you hear yourself? When did you get so interested in my love life or lack thereof?"

"Look, I'm just trying to be a good citizen. There's a recession on. You can't afford to be throwing away perfectly good men," Mona protested. "It's un-American."

"That's it!" Chastain said with a shake of her head. "I'm so through with you. What are you doing tonight?"

"A sorority sister of mine is coming over and we're going to get some Chinese takeout and catch up. I haven't seen her in ages."

"Have fun and don't give Lulu anything with onions in it. She'll beg like crazy, but dogs can't have onions. If you go out, just put her in her crate."

"Yes, Mommy," Mona teased, grinning. "You're still avoiding the issue. Philippe wants an answer to his question, whatever it is, and you're scared he's going to get it."

Chastain frowned just as the buzzer rang signaling David's arrival. "Don't make a nuisance of yourself, Mona. I'll see you ladies later."

They were seated next to the windows of the restaurant, which gave them a view of the park. Everything had an amber glow from the candles and discreet wall sconces. It was a lovely room and Chastain looked like a jewel in the middle of a beautiful setting. The music in the restaurant was as good as the food, but Chastain didn't seem to be paying attention to either. Even when the quintet started playing one of her favorite songs, John Coltrane's "A Love Supreme", she had the same pleasant, distracted look on her face. David reached over the table and took her hand, which made her jump as though she'd been scalded.

"That's not the effect I was hoping for," he said with a half smile.

"I'm sorry, I think my mind was somewhere else," she apologized. She looked at his hand on hers and wondered why she wasn't feeling what a woman normally feels when a handsome man touches her.

"Let me guess what you were thinking about. Or should I say 'who'? You're thinking about Deveraux, aren't you?"

Chastain pulled her hand away from David's and put it in her lap with her other hand. She laced her fingers together and mustered up a smile. "What makes you say that?"

"Maybe because I ran into him when I came into the

gallery," he said. "When I was coming in he was leaving. He'd just bought some art, too." David waited for her reaction, which was immediate.

"He did *what?* Please tell me it wasn't the nudes. I told him they weren't for sale. Honestly, that man is driving me crazy," she said angrily.

David picked up his glass of wine and took a sip. "I didn't say what he purchased. Actually, he bought the Bricktop triptych."

Her face was flushed. David observed her for a moment before speaking. He leaned forward with eyes full of concern. "Why did you think he tried to buy the nudes?"

"Because we talked today," she said candidly. "He came to Studio L and asked if we could have a few minutes alone and we went upstairs where he proposed the ridiculous idea that he buy the paintings. Something along the lines of that if he bought them and took them off the market that the so-called lawsuit would disappear," she replied.

"And I take it you didn't like that idea?"

"Hell no, David, I didn't. They're not for sale at any price, especially not to him."

"Why not?" he asked reasonably. "If he wants them that badly you could name any price and live quite comfortably off the proceeds for some time. You could set up the arts foundation for gifted students in New Orleans that you were talking about. In today's precarious times living well is truly the best revenge. Take his money and run." He was pleased to see her smile, even though it wasn't the usual full-on smile that was so sexy it was blinding.

"That's an idea, David. Not a good one, but it's an idea. But it's completely out of the question."

David drank the rest of his wine. "I'm going to go where no brother has gone before, Chastain. I'm not trying to meddle in your personal affairs, but I think you and Deveraux have some unfinished business."

"What makes you say that, David?"

"It's not just because of the paintings, it's because of the way the two of you were and the way you seem to be now. There's too much that hasn't been resolved with you and Deveraux. You need to have cl—"

"Oh, please don't say I need closure," she said with a shudder. "I hate that word. It's supposed to be the miracle cure for everything—*closure.*"

David laughed, but his face quickly turned serious. "Chastain, I come from a big family. I'm the oldest and I don't like to share. What's mine is mine and I don't give it up easily. That goes for toys, clothes and anything else that was mine. I was known as the selfish one," he admitted. "I still am, at least when it comes to my heart. I can't share. I'm hoping you and I can take it to another level, but as long as you and Deveraux haven't resolved your issues, I don't know how it's going to work."

Chastain turned her face to the windows and watched the fat flakes of snow tumbling down from the night sky. The restaurant had twinkly little white lights everywhere and the quintet started playing "Have

Yourself a Merry Little Christmas." It would have been the perfect moment for her to turn to David and assure him that there were no obstacles and that Philippe was no longer a part of her life. Unfortunately, she was just too honest to do that. She knew deep in her heart that David was absolutely right.

She removed her hands from her lap, placing one on the table and using the other to support her chin as she looked at David forlornly. "I'm sorry, David. I guess I am kind of confused by this whole thing," she admitted.

He took her hand again and squeezed it gently. "You wouldn't be human if you weren't. All of us have some ghosts in our pasts. If I was confronted with a few of mine I have no idea how I'd react. Listen, I have to go out of town for a while. Maybe by the time I get back you'll have a better handle on everything."

"How long will you be gone?"

"Not sure. I have a couple of exhibits to attend and a few meetings with potential clients. I also have to go home to Virginia. My folks are having a big anniversary party." He stroked the soft skin on the back of her hand with his thumb. "But I'll be back by the time your family comes up from Louisiana. I can't wait to meet them," he said.

Chastain nodded. "You're very considerate, David. My family is going to enjoy meeting you."

"I try to be considerate, but let's not forget I don't like to share. I'm giving you a clear field so you can assess your situation with Deveraux. And maybe your family will like me so much it'll tip the scales in my favor," he teased gently.

She smiled. "You never know. What's for dessert?"

"That's more like it," David replied. "I love a woman who loves a good dessert. That means you have a sweet heart. That's what my mother says, something like that."

Chastain gave a real laugh for the first time. "In that case mine must be amazing because I've never met a pastry I didn't like. Let's order two and share," she suggested.

"We can order the entire dessert menu if you'll smile like that all night," he told her. "When you smile it makes me glad I'm a man, Chas."

What could she do after a compliment like that except smile again?

Chapter 8

A few days went by before Chastain spoke to Philippe again and it was because she wouldn't take his calls. He meant it when he said he had her number. He was blowing up her cell like mad. She just wasn't ready to deal with him. It wasn't as if she was in New York on vacation. She had plenty to do. There were more interviews and speaking engagements and other exhibit openings. Plus, she still had friends in the city to hook up with. And she was still inspired to paint. She'd been painting furiously every spare moment when she wasn't tending to Lulu. Mona read her very well and backed off from her usual barrage of questions even though her curiosity was eating her up. But she was smart enough to leave Chastain alone for now.

Chastain had found a small park not too far from the gallery that she took Lulu to. The little Westie was very excited about the snow and she loved running in it, burying her nose in the drifts and making what Chastain called doggie angels by rolling around in it. The sight of Lulu in her red coat running to and fro made Chastain forget about Philippe Deveraux, at least for the duration of their walks. They were headed back to the gallery when Lulu began barking frantically and lunged forward so fast that she jerked the leash out of Chastain's hand. Chastain let out a shriek and ran after Lulu, whose short legs pounded down the wet pavement.

She slowed down when she saw where Lulu was racing. She saw Philippe walking toward Studio L and she knew Lulu was running straight toward him. As Chastain slowed down she went sliding on a patch of ice, lost her balance and landed on a small icy puddle right in front of Philippe.

"Are you hurt?" he asked as he pulled her up with one hand. Lulu was tucked under his arm with a ridiculously happy smile on her snow-covered face.

"Only my ego. The rest of me is just fine," she mumbled.

He held her arm until they were inside when she pulled away. "Thanks for your help. Although it wouldn't have been necessary if someone I know hadn't decided to make a break for it," she said, shaking her finger at Lulu. She held out her hands to take her, but Philippe demurred.

"Let me take her upstairs for you."

Chastain let him since she was wet and icy cold and she wanted to slink up to the loft and change before anyone saw her. When they reached the loft, she took off her hooded brown coat and her boots. Philippe had unhooked Lulu's leash and was about to take her coat off.

"Watch out. She's going to buck like mad because she loves that coat. She hates to take it off," Chastain warned.

Philippe laughed at the sight of her, wriggling and kicking like crazy, but he put a finger between her eyes and spoke firmly. "Sit."

She sat at once and he took off the damp dog wrap. "Where do you want this?"

Chastain made a face. "Little traitor. I chased her for a half hour one day and finally I gave up and she stomped around for about three hours with the stupid thing on. How did you do that? Never mind, I don't want to know. It's probably a man thing or something. Thanks for your help. See you when I see you," she added, walking to the doorway.

Philippe ignored her and looked around the loft. He could see her workspace by the large windows on one wall, and the sleek, minimalist look of the space. But something was missing. "Where's your Christmas tree?"

"My what?"

"Your tree. You don't have one single Christmas decoration, nothing to celebrate the season at all. I'm surprised at you, Chastain. Have you gotten too sophisticated for the holidays?"

She frowned at him. "Christmas isn't my favorite time of year."

"Since when? You always loved it," he countered. "You were like a little kid, always excited and happy about every aspect of it. You used to start decorating on Thanksgiving as I recall."

"Things changed, Philippe. Right about the time you dumped me my senior year of high school. It was just before the precious holiday if you recall."

He looked shocked, then puzzled. "I didn't get rid of you. I said that you should feel free to date when you were in school, that's all. I didn't want you to feel tied down. I wanted you to experience everything in college that any young woman should and if that meant going out with some guy, I didn't want to you feel like you couldn't do that. What made you think I was trying to break up with you?"

Chastain stared at him with suspicious eyes. "You said to date other people. Everybody knows that means you want to break up and that's the convenient way of doing it."

Philippe stroked his goatee with his long fingers. "Okay, we were young and you were inexperienced so I can maybe see how you might have misinterpreted what I said."

"I didn't misinterpret anything. I know what you said and I know what it meant. Look, why don't you get out of here so I can change? My fingers are turning blue," she said tiredly.

"Go take a shower and change. I'm not leaving,

though. We need to talk some more and I need to spend some time with my dog," he answered.

"Excuse me? You gave her to me, remember?"

"I loaned her to you," he corrected. "Get in the shower. Your teeth are starting to chatter and it's not sexy."

"Well, God forbid I shouldn't meet your standards of sexiness," she spat out. She walked to the bathroom as quickly as her wet pants and shivering limbs would allow.

The shower did feel good. She scrubbed her body briskly with a nylon pouf and after she toweled off and put on lots of body cream, she felt better, especially after she put on a pair of thick socks, a lined pair of high-waisted, wide-legged wool trousers and a heavy hand-knit sweater she'd picked up in Ireland. Her hair was carelessly arranged in a curly mass and she skipped makeup except for a little tinted moisturizer and a rosy lip gloss. Now she was ready to shoo Philippe away and get some work done.

To her surprise, Philippe had prepared lunch. He'd taken off his suit coat and tie and rolled up his sleeves. He was stirring something that smelled heavenly on the stovetop and the bar was set for two. "What's all this?"

"It's my world famous grilled cheese sandwiches and a bowl of shrimp bisque. I raided your fridge," he said. "Have a seat."

She did so at once and marveled at the meal he'd prepared. He ladled the soup in two big bowls and put a thick, golden brown sandwich on each plate. They said grace and Chastain dug in. The bisque was delicious. It had bits of turkey bacon as well as a generous helping of tiny shrimp and it was thick with butter and cream. The sandwich was made with Gruyere and boursin cheese on the slightly chewy artisanal bread she loved. The outside was crisp and golden and the inside was melting and gooey. She had eaten quite a bit before she noticed that Philippe was devouring his meal.

"When did you start eating meat and dairy? I thought you were a vegan for life," she said.

He shrugged. "After Katrina things changed. When I saw people fighting for their lives and the lives of their families and neighbors, survival took on a different meaning for me. I was at an elderly lady's house after the storm and she had cooked a special meal for the volunteers and I couldn't disappoint her by not eating. It just didn't seem quite as important when people were offering to share what little they had with me."

"You've changed, Philippe."

"As have you. We're older and wiser and shaped by our experiences," he said.

"No, I mean it," she said. "You really have changed. Like my nonexistent Christmas decorations, for instance. You always said they weren't environmentally friendly and were wasteful. But the first thing you pointed out was that I don't have any. That's a big change for you. And I never thought I'd see the day when you ate meat or anything close to it again."

"I've been to Africa, Haiti and lots of other places where there is famine and poverty like you wouldn't believe. I got over myself. When someone offered me something to eat, I ate it whether it was a fried beetle or a roasted scorpion. I didn't want to embarrass anybody. And for the record, I still don't eat much meat. I eat very little but I enjoy every bite."

"I'm enjoying my lunch. I'd forgotten how well you cook."

"You've forgotten a few other things, too," he said.

"Like what? Don't be cryptic, I'm not up for it," she said. Lulu patted her leg politely with her forepaw, waiting for a taste. Chastain broke off a thumbnail sized morsel and fed it to her.

"You're forgetting that you broke it off with me at Christmastime, too. The last Christmas you spent in New Orleans," he reminded her.

Chastain was giving Lulu another crumb of sandwich and she almost fell off her stool. "Philippe, you really need to stay off the pipe," she said. "Whatever you've been smoking has warped your brain. I didn't break anything off with you, *you* dumped *me* for the second time," she said angrily.

"Excuse you? You picked the most romantic, sexy night in the world, a night that just happened to be Christmas Eve, to tell me that somebody had just thrown a load of cash at you and you were gonna jump the pond to study and grow and contemplate your damned navel or something. That's called dumping someone, Chastain, look it up. In general when you leave town for an extended period, you're breaking up. But when you leave town, state, country and continent, it's pretty much a given that you don't want to see the other person again."

Lulu barked anxiously because she didn't like the sounds her people were making. Chastain got off her stool and picked her up. "It's okay, sweetie. Nobody's mad at you. Your daddy is exhibiting signs of a psychotic break, that's all. He's a little mental," she said, narrowing her eyes at Philippe.

"And for the record, you were the one who didn't care if I went to France or Mars or Timbuktu. If you wanted me to stay in New Orleans with you all you had to do was say so and I was listening very hard that night, Philippe. I didn't hear a word that sounded like 'stay with me.'"

Philippe stood up and took two steps and he was in front of her. He put his hands on her shoulders and looked at her with a mixture of anger and desire. "Then you need to listen carefully. I want you to stay with me, Chastain. I want you to spend Christmas with me."

Lulu barked and waved her paws. Apparently it sounded like a good idea to her, but Chastain was too stunned to speak.

Chapter 9

Chastain's head was reeling as she pushed Lulu into Philippe's arms. She walked away from him and went to the windows, leaning her forehead against the cool glass. "You really have lost your mind, haven't you?"

Philippe put Lulu on the floor and she ran over to join Chastain, jumping onto the window seat to look, too, in case there was a bird or something else bark-worthy. He came into the living room, but he went to her easel to look at her work. "No, Cerise, I haven't lost anything but time with you. This is the perfect solution to our problem."

She turned to face him, leaning her back against the glass. "What problem is that? I don't have a problem," she said.

"No, we do," he replied. "This is beautiful, by the way, just like everything you paint. I'm humbled by your talent."

"Don't go there, buddy. That's not making me think you're less crazy."

Philippe started walking toward her with his hands in his pockets. "We've been laboring under a few misconceptions here. You think I was kicking you to the curb and I think you ran out on me. If we had been mature enough to think with our heads and not our hearts, we could have made it work."

He was in front of her now, looming over her so closely that she could smell his skin, the uniquely clean smell that was all him without artifice or cologne. "All I'm asking is a chance to put things back together. You stay with me through the Christmas holidays and if you haven't changed your mind about us we'll call it a day once and for all."

Chastain moved so that she wasn't in danger of being pinned to the cold window by Philippe. Her arms were crossed tightly and she was glaring at him. He went on talking as though she wasn't looking at him with disdain.

"We need this, Cerise. We have too much unfinished business to let it go."

Her expression went blank. "That's what David said."

Philippe raised one thick eyebrow. "I'm going to have to take back some of the things I've been saying about him. He's a smart man, Cerise, but he really has nothing to do with this conversation or this situation. We have to do this for us, no one else."

"Philippe, what makes you think I haven't already moved on mentally and emotionally? You're wading into some seriously unknown territory here."

He didn't answer right away. Instead he extended his index finger and put it behind her ear. He was barely touching her as he ran his finger down her neck. Her breathing changed almost imperceptibly. Only someone who knew her as well as he did could have heard the tiny sigh that escaped her lips. She leaned toward him and put her hand on his waist while he slowly drew her into his arms. When she was so close that they could feel each other's heartbeats, he bent his head to hers until their lips touched.

Philippe's mouth touched hers gently at first, but her consent signaled more. Chastain opened her mouth slightly, enough to run her tongue along his lower lip and gently pull it into her mouth, while he did the same to her upper lip. The tentative probing turned into a long sensual exploration that showed no sign of ending. They kissed until they were devouring each other, trying to satisfy the hungry desire that had been aroused. Chastain tried to pull away from him but he persisted, lifting her off the floor and anchoring her to his hips.

"You have to stop," she murmured.

"I don't think I can," he whispered. "Cerise, you taste so good I don't want to let you go."

The elevator sprang into action, which was enough

to make him reluctantly end the kiss. When her feet were on the floor again, he kissed her forehead as he tilted her chin so he could look into her passion-filled eyes.

"This is how I know we aren't finished, Cerise. Will you stay with me for Christmas?"

A voice she barely recognized answered him. "Yes."

"You are one fab chica, Chastain. I'm loving that LBD," praised Mona. She stood in the doorway of Chastain's bedroom watching her put the finishing touch on her ensemble. "Where are you going, again?"

"He's taking me to Zazu's. It's fairly new and it's supposed to be really good," she said. "That's why I'm wearing my little black dress. Maybe somebody will think I'm a chic New Yorker." She was holding an earring to each lobe, trying to decide which one to wear. Her dress had bracelet sleeves with a boat neckline in front and a very low back. The bodice of the dress was wool jersey and the bottom was crepe-backed satin that was cut in a circle to sway gracefully around her knees. With her black pumps and a black belt with a jeweled buckle, she looked gorgeous.

"Your waist is so small," Mona said wistfully. "I'm so jealous."

"Jealous of what? Everyone isn't meant to be scrawny like me. And if you want to meet Wade, you need to stay just the way you are. He likes something to hold, honey." Mona was anything but fat. She was just a healthy size fourteen or sixteen, depending on the designer. Chastain had decided to go with the black pearl earrings and now she was selecting a necklace. The one she chose was a small diamond circle intersected on each side with a thin gold chain. She touched it with her finger and smiled before turning around to face Mona. "Anything out of order?"

"You look perfect. Philippe won't know what hit him."

"That's the idea. I'm trying to keep him off guard so he can't overwhelm me. I'm not convinced that this in my best interests," she said.

"I think it's romantic," Mona sighed. "Spending Christmas together in New York. What could be better than that? And I like the fact that he's starting out slowly. You've been to lunch with him and to a play and now you're going to a fancy restaurant. How did he manage to get a table at Zazu's, anyway? I hear it's booked for months."

"His cousin, Ricki, is married to the owner, so no problem." At the sound of the elevator Chastain smiled. "Lulu, I think that's your daddy. Go get him."

Philippe was indeed on the elevator and Lulu greeted him with her usual enthusiasm. He and Mona chatted until Chastain made her entrance at which point the conversation stopped, at least for him.

"Cerise, you're gorgeous."

Mona couldn't resist a question. "Why do you call her Cerise?"

Philippe and Chastain locked eyes and laughed. "Sorry, Mona, it's just too private to share," she said.

Philippe held up her black coat and while she was slipping her arms into the sleeves he pressed a kiss on the back of her neck. "Don't start something you can't finish," she warned him.

"Don't challenge me. You know I won't back down," he countered.

"I'm not saying another word until I'm fed."

"Your wish is my command. Let's go." They stepped into the elevator holding hands.

Mona picked up Lulu. "Come with me, little girl. Let's watch a movie and you can sleep with me while your people are off bein' grown and sexy. They think I don't know where that name came from, but I do. *'Cerise'* means cherry and that means he picked hers. I am scared of them," she told the dog.

Zazu's wasn't a large restaurant, but it was spectacular. It was very intimate, with bamboo tables, indigo draperies and carpeting and lighting that made it intimate without being too dark. Chastain looked around the room with pleasure.

"This place is just wonderful, Philippe. Ricki's husband must be very proud of it."

"You can ask him yourself, Cerise. Here he comes."

Antoine was making his way across the dining room, stopping to talk to and be greeted by his guests, some of whom were Broadway stars, athletes and celebrities. He was tall and fit with a head of thick, wavy, dark hair that was a marked contrast to his pale olive complexion. His hazel eyes showed admiration when Philippe introduced him to Chastain. He bowed and kissed her hand.

"You are *magnifique,* my dear. So lovely and talented. It's a real pleasure to meet you. Ricki has not stopped talking about you since you two met. And your puppy made quite an impression on my littlest one. She has been babbling about dogs every day since then. I'm afraid there's a puppy in my future," he said, smiling.

Chastain beamed. It was impossible not to like him. He was so personable and charming. She thanked him for the compliment and paid him one of her own.

"Your restaurant is simply gorgeous," she told him.

He looked pleased. "I am going to prepare your meal myself and it's not on the menu. Tonight you will have your own *spécialité de la maison,*" he said. "I hope you like *fruits de la mer.*"

Chastain assured him that she loved seafood.

He waved and said they would be dining shortly. "And when you come to our house, we'll have something really special," he promised her.

He was gone before Chastain could ask him what he meant by that, but Philippe explained. "Ricki has been dying to have you over so we're going there tomorrow. Does that work for you?"

A few days ago she would have given him a snarky response but she just nodded and agreed. "I really enjoy talking to Ricki. She reminds me of your sister. Their children must be adorable."

"If that's a code word for savages, then yes, they are," he joked. "They're very good kids, but when you have five of them, the noise level rises exponentially depending on what they're doing."

Their meal was as good as Antoine promised. It started with watercress soup, spicy and soothing to the tongue. Then lobster medallions grilled in butter and finished with white wine and herbs served on a bed of baby arugula. Pan-seared scallops served with crimini mushrooms followed the first course. They were served tender asparagus and crab ravioli with a Pernod cream sauce sprinkled with finely chopped angelica. When it was time for dessert, Chastain simply didn't have room. Antoine insisted that she take it home. It was a dark chocolate gateau made with ground pistachios instead of flour and covered with ganache and garnished with raspberries. He gave her the entire cake in a gold Zazu's box tied with indigo ribbon. Chastain was totally blissed-out by the experience.

Philippe had hired a limo to drive them, which was totally unlike him, but very welcome. They were sitting in the back of the limo behind the soundproof divider.

"I know I said this before, but this limo is wonderful. It's such a luxury," she said, sighing. "If I didn't know better I'd think you were trying to impress me," she teased.

"I am. I want to dazzle you, Cerise. Why are you so far away?"

She smiled mischievously. "Because I'm going to make you work really hard, Mr. Deveraux. I'm not cheap, nor am I easy."

"No, you aren't. You're priceless and very difficult, but I'm not afraid of hard work. Let me show you what I mean."

He held out his hand and pulled her into his lap.

Chapter 10

Chastain giggled as Philippe held her tightly. "That was nothing. Where's all that hard work you were talking about?"

He made a low growling sound and took her lips with his own while sliding his hand under her coat. He stroked her bare back and she arched into him as the sensation ignited a fire in her. His tongue explored her mouth and hers returned the favor while a low melodic moan grew deep in her throat.

"When you make that sound it drives me crazy," he said with a husky rasp.

"Take me home and you can hear it longer and louder," she purred.

Ten minutes later they entered the elevator at

Studio L. "I don't think I like this arrangement," Philippe said thoughtfully. "How often do you go in and out of here at night?"

Chastain was standing on tiptoe, kissing his neck. "It's perfectly safe here, darling. There are lights outside, security cameras and a security guard. I lived in New York for years. I'm very street smart."

"I didn't see a security guard," Philippe grumbled.

"He's making the rounds of the building. There's a warehouse on the second floor. Do you mind shutting up? I'm trying to be seductive," she pouted.

Philippe kissed her without warning as he scooped her up in his arms. They kissed all the way up to the loft until Philippe slowly let her down so she could stand on her own feet. She put the cake on the counter and before he could take her coat off, Lulu came out of Mona's bedroom.

"Hello there. Mona's letting you sleep with her, hmm? You're so spoiled!" Chastain retrieved a little chew treat and gave it to her.

Philippe hadn't taken his coat off. He came up behind her and put his hands on her shoulders. "Cerise, I'm going to get going."

She leaned back against his hard muscular length. "Why? Don't you want some of that sinful cake?"

"Yes, I do. I want to take that sexy dress off your gorgeous body and lay you down so I can take that cake and smear it all over you and then eat it off of your body very slowly. But not here and not tonight."

She turned around to look at him. "You'd better have a good reason."

"I have more than one. We're not alone, for one thing, and this place belongs to another man, for another. We need privacy and I need exclusivity. So this weekend I'm taking you somewhere so we can have both. Sounds okay?"

Chastain loved looking up at him. He was so tall and gorgeous and his eyes were the sexiest things in the world to look into. "Sounds fine."

"Then I'll pick you and Lulu up for lunch with Ricki and Antoine and their little monsters and afterward we're off for the weekend. Can you hold out until then?"

She held up one finger. "Just one more kiss and I might be able to hold out."

He put his hands around her waist and lifted her up while she wrapped her arms around his neck. After a long, satisfying kiss, he gently let her slide down to the floor. He played with Lulu for a minute and kissed Chastain quickly before he left.

It would only be a day before they went away, but Chastain didn't think she could wait.

Chastain's eyes widened when she saw the size of the apartment building where Ricki lived. "This looks like that building in *Rosemary's Baby,*" she said. "It's huge."

"It's remodeled inside so the interior is not so Gothic. They live in the penthouse," he said.

It was true, the lobby area was elegantly furnished and nothing resembled a medieval dungeon. Once they were in the mirrored elevator, Philippe smiled down at her. "Have I told you how pretty you look today?"

Chastain smiled back. "Are you talking to me or your girlfriend?" Lulu was tucked under his arm wearing a perky green sweater he'd bought her.

"To Lulu, of course. The word pretty doesn't even begin to describe you."

"Thank you, Philippe," she said.

They were both dressed casually, Philippe in jeans and Chastain in charcoal gray trousers. He was wearing a beautiful mahogany brown sweater and she had on an unusual sweater the same color as her pants. It was made by an avant-garde Japanese designer. It had an asymmetrical neckline and hemline and resembled a deconstructed kimono. She'd blown her hair dry and used a flat iron to bump it out. She wore a little diamond necklace and big hoop earrings.

The elevator to the penthouse floor opened to a hall with three doors. Philippe went to the middle one, using his key to open it. "Anybody home?" he called out.

"Of course we are," Ricki answered. She was in the living room surrounded by some of the most adorable children Chastain had ever seen.

"Come in, come in!" She rose from the sofa and held out her hands to Chastain. They hugged while the children gathered around to meet Lulu.

"She's very friendly and she never bites. But she

will lick you if you let her. Be very gentle with her, okay?" Philippe looked at each child in turn. "Introduce yourselves to Miss Chastain," he instructed.

The older of the two little girls spoke right up. She was apparently the leader of the group. "I'm Jennifer, and I'm the oldest. This is my twin brother Jacques."

"But aren't you the same age?" Chastain asked with a smile.

"Yes, we're both nine but I was born ten minutes before he was. This is Paul and he's seven, and this is Dominic who is five and this is our baby, Demetria. She's three, so she's almost a little girl, but she's still the baby." She took a breath before adding, "You're very pretty."

"Thank you, honey. So are you," Chastain replied. "Ricki, your children are just beautiful. If you ever want a family portrait, let me know."

"Bless your heart, of course I do. I'm so glad you mentioned it so I didn't have to beg. I would have, you know."

Philippe took her coat and Lulu's. Lulu was so excited about having children to play with she let him take off her sweater without a struggle. She loved being the center of attention and she played quite nicely with them. Of course it all came to a halt when Antoine came into the room. Lulu went to him at once and stood up with her most beguiling expression.

"So this is the little dog that Demetria keeps talking about? I can see why she was so impressed." He started talking to Lulu in French and laughed when she seemed to understand him.

"She is definitely bilingual," Chastain said. "We lived in France for three years. Watch this." She took something out of her purse and held out her hand. "*Pomme*. Lulu, *pomme*."

Lulu stopped doting on Antoine and ran over to get the little piece of apple Chastain was holding. "She loves apples. I always bring treats with me," she said sheepishly.

"All good mommies do," Ricki laughed. "Look at my crew and imagine how many baggies of Cheerios, muesli and baby carrots I've toted around. I still have one for the baby." She linked her arm with Chastain's and said, "Let's go in the kitchen. I'm supposed to be sous-chef today and I've been slacking off," she confessed.

Chastain looked around while Antoine led them to the kitchen. The living and dining rooms were furnished beautifully in shades of buttery yellow and gold with cream and green accents. The rooms were wonderful, French country yet chic, but the kitchen was astounding.

There was a dark green four-oven Aga range, the best oven made in England. Next to it was a huge grill that could accommodate enough food for a football team. A big stainless steel work island topped by a large pot rack dominated the area in the center of the room. There was a double-sided Sub-Zero refrigerator with a glass front on one side and stainless steel on the other. There was also a deep triple sink and a restaurant-style faucet and sprayer and two dishwashers.

The most amazing part of the kitchen to Chastain was the fireplace on the opposite wall. There was a comfortable eating nook, which looked so cozy and country she almost expected to hear the sound of livestock. Even though Antoine had been cooking a big meal, the kitchen was as neat and orderly as only a professional chef could manage and the smells that were coming from the range were so appetizing her stomach began to growl.

"This is the most wonderful kitchen I've ever seen in my life," she said. "My grandmother would flip out if she saw this. She's owned a restaurant for like a million years and I don't think the kitchen at Mama T's is this large."

"Didn't you tell me your family is coming next week for the exhibit? Bring them over. Antoine likes to talk food. His favorite people in the world are chefs," she said.

Antoine stopped stirring and came over to kiss his wife. "*Non, cherie,* you are my favorite people, you and our babies. Is anyone getting hungry?"

Antoine had made a traditional French meal of pâté and coq au vin. The chicken with wine and vegetables was deliciously filling with the crusty bread also made by Antoine. They ate in the kitchen at a large trestle table made of reclaimed oak. Everyone enjoyed the meal, the children especially. Remarkably, Antoine admitted that they had never had fast food in their lives.

"Everything they eat is prepared by me or Ricki. If you give them good food they know what it is supposed to taste like and they won't eat the junk."

Even Lulu got to share in the meal. Antoine gave her a plate of finely chopped pâté and she enjoyed it thoroughly. He was quite taken with the little Westie so when the children asked when they would get a dog of their own, he and Ricki looked at each other and he answered, "Soon, if we can find one as nice as this one. Where did you get her, Chastain?"

Chastain put her hand over Philippe's and told them that Philippe had rescued her and her two puppies during Katrina. "She's a very tough lady. She managed to keep her puppies alive during the worst of the flooding. If you get a dog, you might want to see if you can get one that was rescued, like Miss Tallulah here. She was so grateful to be taken in she's just been a joy. Philippe gave one puppy to his niece, and the other one to his sister-in-law. And he loaned Lulu to me because I was living alone in the Quarter after the storm." She looked at him with a sweet smile. "One of the best gifts he ever gave me," she said.

"Are Westies good around children?" Ricki asked. "I can see that Lulu is, but what about in general?"

"They are, but they're very stubborn and they will do what you want them to do when they want to do it. You might want to think about a bigger dog, like a Lab. They're very patient and kind and they don't feel the need to bark like a terrier. My friend Jan has four Labs and I've never heard a bark out of any of them. Lulu can woof the house down," she admitted.

Jennifer suddenly piped up and asked a question. "Does Lulu play with your children?"

Chastain looked confused. "What children, honey?"

"Your children with cousin Philippe. Don't you have children?"

"Um, no," she replied quickly.

"But you're married, aren't you?" asked Paul. "You look married."

Chastain glanced at Philippe who was looking perfectly at ease. She wanted to pop him in the back of his head, but there was more that followed from the precocious twins.

"When you're married you have to have children," Jacques explained. "That's your legacy."

Chastain was too through. She was ready to slide under the table from embarrassment. Philippe just smiled and asked Jacques what legacy meant.

Jennifer answered for him. "Cousin Philippe, it's all you have to carry on your name. You should know that. My papa told us all about it," she said confidently.

Ricki, God bless her, decided to change the subject. "I love that necklace. I've been looking for something like that for the girls when they get a little older. Where did you find it?"

"It was a gift from Philippe," she answered faintly.

"See? You only take jewelry from your husband," Jennifer said. "Or from your papa, isn't that right, Papa?"

"They must be married," Dominic said. "May we have some tarte, Mama?"

Ricki nodded her head in exasperation. "Absolutely. If it will keep you from talking, you certainly may."

It was a nice try on her part but a little late, Chastain thought as Philippe nearly choked trying not to laugh out loud at his young cousins.

Chapter 11

Philippe made sure the door was double-locked before turning around. He gave Chastain a secretive smile. "Guess what we are," he asked.

She looked around the living room of the luxurious hotel suite quizzically. "I'm just guessing here, but I think we're in a very expensive suite in the W Hotel," she said. "What else?"

He took off his coat as he walked across the room. "We're alone," he said dramatically. "You and I are all alone, just the two of us, for the first time in more than three years."

Lulu stopped her meticulous investigation of the room and barked indignantly. Philippe and Chastain both laughed at the look she was giving him. "I'm sorry, sweetie, you're here, too. And Daddy got you a nice little bed to sleep in so you can stay in the living room and we can have some privacy."

After lunch with Rickie and Antoine, they had gone shopping. Philippe had gotten Lulu a very stylish doggie bed with four posters and a canopy. It was black with leopard-patterned trim and hot pink accents and Chastain had begged him not to get it.

"It looks like something a Bourbon street call girl would sleep on. It's way over-the-top, Philippe."

"Exactly," he answered. "She'll love it."

He'd bought a couple of toys, too, and had it all delivered to the W. Chastain could see that he'd had a few other things delivered. The W hotel chain was known for its "whatever, whenever" service and Philippe had taken full advantage. There were flowers on the coffee table, but they were silk, fabulously fashioned and very realistic. He knew that she loved flowers but hated cut ones so it was a sweet gesture on his part. She also saw bottles of raspberry spumante on the bar, another sweet gesture because he knew she disliked alcohol.

"Philippe, this is too much," she protested softly. Lulu didn't seem to think so after she found her favorite treat on the coffee table. She stood on her hind legs and helped herself to the little silver bowl that was heaped with them. He'd had the bowl sent over from Tiffany's along with matching dishes for food and water.

"It's not enough, Cerise. This is called making up for lost time," he said as he draped his arms over her shoulders. "We've been apart for too long."

His lips felt wonderful on her skin as he kissed her forehead. A soft sound of utter contentment came from her throat as she leaned into him. Her head tilted back to receive his mouth but it never came. Lulu was jumping up and down and making angry noises. They both started laughing at the sight of her.

"I think she's jealous," Chastain said. "I've never seen her do that before."

Philippe grinned. "So that means she's never seen you getting busy. Nice to know," he said with amused satisfaction.

Chastain shrugged her way out of his arms. "So you say. I'm going to take a bath. You two have fun," she said as she walked toward the bedroom. She could hear his deep voice as he cajoled Lulu into her new bed. *Good luck on that,* she thought. No creature on earth could be as stubborn as a West Highland White Terrier when it wanted to be. She went into the bathroom, marveling at the size and depth of the tub. Once the water was running, she went back to the bedroom to hang up the rest of her clothes. To her surprise, Philippe was there, taking off his shirt.

"What are you doing? Where's Lulu?"

"Lulu is curled up on her nice bed with her new toy. I put a CD in for her and she's quite happy. I'm getting undressed because I believe strongly in water conservation and I'm getting in the bathtub with you," he said.

Chastain was momentarily stunned into silence by the sight of his broad chest and tight, muscular abs. He looked the same, but even better than she remembered.

She could recall exactly how the thick hair on his chest felt against her naked breasts and a sudden burst of moisture blossomed between her legs. He'd taken off his shoes and socks and was unbuckling his belt when he spoke again.

"Cerise, are you okay? You look like you're somewhere else. If you don't want me to get in with you, just say so."

"Did I say that? I don't think I said anything of the kind," she murmured. "You're going awfully fast," she added. "Take my sweater off, please."

He did so at once. "I was planning on it. I love to undress you, Cerise."

The soft knit sweater slipped off easily and she watched the passion mount in his eyes as he beheld her breasts displayed in a sheer lace and satin bra. It was so delicate it didn't seem capable of providing any kind of support, but what it lacked in practicality it more than made up for in utter sexiness. It was a pretty shade of lilac because she knew he liked purple.

His pants came off as well as hers and in one quick move Philippe had them lying across the enormous bed. "I might look the same but you don't," he murmured.

Chastain was stung by his words. "I do, too," she protested. "What do you mean?"

He was propped up on his elbow, leaning over her while his free hand stroked her all over. "You were always pretty," he told her. "From the first time I saw you with the pigtails and the glasses and the bony legs, you were always the prettiest girl in the room wherever you were."

Chastain wanted to answer him but his hand was under her thong and his fingers were stroking her womanhood in long lazy motions that were making her shake with need.

"When we started dating, you were even prettier than you were then," he said before taking her mouth in a deep kiss. His tongue and his finger were moving in sync, the twin pressures causing her to rotate her hips and flex her fingers on the silk jacquard duvet that covered the bed. "I loved everything about you," he told her between kisses. "Your face, your eyes, your hair and your skin," he said. "Your skin is softer than anything I've ever touched."

He bent his head to her breasts and she undid the front hook that allowed him access to her nipples, which were already tight and hard, waiting for his touch. When he took one in his mouth and lavished it with his tongue she moaned his name, a deep purr that signaled the beginning of her release. He had two fingers deep inside her and his thumb was stroking her clitoris while he sucked and nibbled her nipple. The twin sensations made her breathe erratically and her hips move frantically until an amazing orgasm shook her body.

"That's what I'm talking about, Cerise. You look so beautiful I almost don't recognize you." He took off her thong and his briefs followed it. He turned over on his back and took her with him so she was on top of him.

She sighed as their bodies met. Hers was still flickering with tremors from the force of the climax she'd just had. Philippe was stroking her up and down, touching her with such skilled passion that she thought she might melt. He kept talking to her as he touched her willing body. "Somewhere along the line you've gone from being gorgeous to being absolutely exquisite. I think you're some kind of siren," he said.

She giggled and then sighed. "No, I'm not. I'm the same goofy kid, Philippe. I just use better cosmetics."

He was fondling her round, firm behind as she spoke and he gave it a squeeze. He held her hips as he began to enter her, sliding his hard manhood into her hot flesh, wet with her desire for him. "What you have doesn't come in a bottle, tube or jar. Let's agree to disagree for now. We've got some other things to concentrate on," he groaned as she raised her body to straddle his. She moved up and down on his massive erection and once a rhythm was established they began to rock and ride until they were both sweaty and satisfied. She leaned forward so he was pressing against her most sensitive parts and she tightened her vaginal walls around him so she could pump his manhood until the inevitable climax claimed them both.

She wanted nothing more than to lie in his arms forever, but he had other plans. "Hold on to me, baby. If we don't get in that tub it's going to overflow."

She locked her arms around his neck and when he stood up, she wrapped her legs around his waist and they went into the bathroom with him still buried inside her. They managed to get there just in time; the tub was full of bubbles but it hadn't overflowed and there was plenty of room for them both. They pulled apart reluctantly so they could get in the soothing water.

"I didn't know you were coming in or I wouldn't have put in the bubble bath," Chastain said with a smile.

"Who cares? Now we'll both smell good. Come here and kiss me, woman."

She knelt between his legs and began a sensuous assault on his lips. It was his turn to groan with pleasure as she took his manhood in both her hands. "Hand me the bath gel, *cher*."

He picked up the tube and took off the top, handing it over with a look of pure satisfaction. "You haven't called me that in so long," he commented. "Sometimes I wondered if I'd ever hear it from you again."

She squeezed the tube to release some of the fragrant gel onto the hand that was still wrapped around him. "That means you must have thought about me from time to time." Putting the tube on the side of the tub, she began to use her supple fingers to gently massage him, smoothing the lather up and down, stroking him into an even higher level of arousal.

"From time to time? I thought about you every day we were apart," he muttered. "That feels good, Cerise."

"I can make it feel better," she crooned. Using her cupped hands to rinse off the lather, she gave him a sultry look. "Are you up to it?"

He slid down so that his head was resting on the bath pillow. "I told you not to challenge me," he drawled.

She looked at the level of the water and frowned. "I think I spoke too soon. I might drown if I do what I'm planning."

He held out his hands to her. "Then we'll wait until we're back in bed. In the meantime, let me bathe you. Turn around and lie back."

She did so and soon his hands were bringing her bliss.

"Is this the way you remember it, Cerise?" Bathing together was one of their favorite things to do once upon a time.

"It's the same but it's brand-new, too," she said.

"It's only going to get better, I promise you. When we get out of the bath, I'm going to show you what I mean."

She couldn't answer because his long fingers had just taken her to another level of pleasure and he drowned her scream with his tongue.

Chapter 12

Philippe meant what he said to Chastain. He had every intention of making love to her until she didn't remember any of the pain of being apart, because he had no intention of ever letting her go again. After their long sensual bath, they toweled each other off and he carried her into the bedroom. They had never been shy about nudity in the past and that hadn't changed. He removed her towel so he could look at her and she acted as though it was the most natural thing in the world.

"I wasn't kidding when I said you've gotten more beautiful, Cerise. What did you do to that cute booty of yours?"

She looked over her shoulder to see her reflection in the mirror. "What are you talking about?"

He stood in front of her and palmed her behind, running his hands over the perfect globes while he looked at her hungrily. "I mean it's always been cute but now it's outstanding, baby. Your hips are a little bigger, too."

"It's just from exercise. I've been working out for years," she murmured.

Philippe was too busy enjoying the view to answer her. She deftly undid his towel and let it drop to the floor and the need for conversation ceased. Chastain walked to the bed with a slow and very sexy walk. His eyes lit up and he asked, "Hey, Cerise, can you still do that thing you used to do?"

By way of answer her buttocks started moving up and down. First the right cheek, then the left one, up and down in the delightful dance that was a direct invitation. "Damn, Cerise. You're the only woman I know who can do that.

She kept doing her little booty dance as she turned down the bed. "Are you coming?" she asked provocatively.

He was across the room in three steps. Once they were both in bed he reached for her and she went into his arms for a long, languorous kiss.

"I love kissing you," she whispered. "Yours was the first kiss I ever enjoyed."

He laughed softly. "I'm honored." He licked her lower lip as he teased her lips apart to deepen the kiss into a mating dance of tongue on tongue. He kissed his way down her neck to her breasts, massaging one while he sucked and licked the other. His tongue traced a pattern down to her navel. Her back was arched and her nipples were huge, which let him know she was experiencing the same kind of pleasure that he was, but he wanted to give her more. He wanted to let her know that she was his in the most intimate way possible.

After kissing her navel he continued making a path down her body to the treasure that waited for him between the satiny skin of her thighs. He rose to his knees and guided her legs over his shoulders. He supported her slight weight with his hands as his mouth sought the source of her womanhood. He tongued her with excruciating slowness until she was moaning and crying his name. After he tasted all of her, he concentrated on the most sensitive part, the ripe pearl that was pulsing and wet for him. She tasted sweeter than cherries and he couldn't stop drinking that sweetness. His tongue didn't stop when he felt her hips moving or when the warm gush of liquid let him know that she had her first climax. He kept going until he knew she was satisfied, after she'd had two more releases and she was holding a pillow over her face to muffle her screams of ecstasy.

He finally relented and stroked her legs as he removed them gently from his shoulders. When they were once again face-to-face on the bed, he couldn't resist teasing her. "I think the walls are pretty much soundproof, Cerise."

She leaned over and kissed him, licking his lips and sucking them gently. "I'm not taking a chance. I don't want to have to explain what we were doing after someone calls the police," she said, laughing.

"If you weren't so loud it wouldn't be a problem," he drawled. "You always were a noisy lover. Ouch," he added as she sank her fingernails into the thicket of his chest hair and tugged gently.

"That's what you get," she said. "And you aren't the one to be talking about somebody being loud. You bring the house down."

She shut him up with another luscious kiss. Her kisses went from his mouth to his chin to his neck. Her hands smoothed his chest and moved to his sides as she circled his nipple with her moist, hot tongue. His eyes closed and he could feel himself getting harder and more aroused with every touch of her hands, every kiss from her sweet mouth. When she finished with his nipples, she kept going lower, finally taking him into her hands.

Her hands felt wonderful, but the first touch of her mouth made his abs tighten. She licked him as if he was a popsicle on a hot day. When she took him into her mouth he felt a surge of love for her that was incredible. She looked so damned sexy with her tousled hair and her pretty lips surrounding him. She sucked him and stroked him and licked him until he was the one biting the pillow. He had to make her stop or he was going to explode all over her face.

"Cerise, baby, mmm, baby, damn," he said hoarsely. She finally stopped and was about to kiss her way up his body but he couldn't wait. He turned her onto her back and entered her with a hard thrust born of his urgent need. The sound that came from deep inside her was all he needed to hear; it was the sound he knew signaled happiness. He thrust again and again as she wrapped her legs around his neck. She was so tight, so hot and wet that it was almost like an out-of-body experience. He looked at her face, flushed and happy, with her eyes closed and her mouth slightly open. He watched her face change as her climax began and he could feel her inner walls clenching and unclenching as she brought him to the brink. His hips stopped moving and his arms tightened around her while the waves of release took them over.

They lay together, still joined because neither one of them wanted to break the connection. Philippe always loved this part of making love to Chastain. This was the point where he'd be ready to leave some other woman's bed, but never with his Cerise. This was just the beginning of what he wanted to share with her.

Sometime later, after more loving and a shared shower, they were cuddled together in front of the fireplace finishing the delicious meal Philippe had had delivered to the suite. He'd put in one of her favorite CDs by Paul Potts and her eyes were closed as she listened to "Nessun Dorma," a truly beautiful aria.

"I love this," she said. "I love music, period. Zydeco, of course, and blues and jazz and R&B, but there's something about opera that just gets to me."

"I know. I listen to quite a bit of it myself."

Her eyes opened in surprise. "Since when? You used to say it sounded like eight cats getting hit in the head with a suitcase."

Philippe gave her the devastating smile that always took her breath away. "It reminded me of you. After you went away I got into it because it was like a connection to you."

She was so touched she wanted to cry, but she caught herself. "Lulu likes it, too. Look at her," she said.

She was lying flat on the carpet like a miniature bearskin rug and she looked totally wrapped up in the music.

"One day I was watching my *Phantom of the Opera* DVD," she recalled, "and Lulu was racing around like her tail was on fire. Emmy Rossum started singing and Lulu stopped dead in her tracks. She sat down and started watching the movie and she didn't move until it was over. She has good taste." She laughed.

"It's because she's a lady, like you," Philippe said. "Here, Lulu." He held out a bit of cantaloupe to her. She turned her head and looked highly disappointed before flopping down again. "Well, I guess she told me."

Chastain laughed. "You don't understand the snack hierarchy. If there's a cracker, she won't eat a dog treat. If there's a cookie, she won't eat a cracker. If there's meat, she won't eat a cookie. But if there's chicken, she won't eat meat. And remember that cheese trumps everything. She'll snatch a piece of cheese out of your mouth if she can. She also likes apples, but if you're putting peanut butter on your apple slices, she has to have it, too."

"Good God, she's rotten," he said.

"You have no idea. You also have to limit her people food or she'll go on strike for her dog food. And don't bother getting her the cute kind with the little dog on it that looks like her. She won't eat it."

Philippe stretched out on the floor, still watching Lulu and Chastain like they were works of art. "You take better care of that dog than some people take of their children."

"I wish I could say you were exaggerating, but you're not. She's my baby," she said simply.

"That means you're going to be an excellent mother," he said thoughtfully.

"What makes you think so? I might just turn into an eccentric old lady with twenty high-strung little dogs yapping around." She got up to put the empty dishes on the room service trolley.

"I can do that," Philippe said. "Or you can just leave it. They'll take care of it."

"I can't stand clutter," she answered. "And I don't like to smell food while I'm trying to sleep. And Lulu is quite capable of treating this like her personal buffet and it'll be a disaster."

She was busy while she was talking and in a couple of minutes she was done. Philippe apologized for his lazy behavior. "I should have helped you, but I'm enjoying the view too much. I've been looking at your legs," he admitted.

Chastain struck a sexy pose for him. While he was wearing a very nice robe without a stitch under it, she was wearing a delightful confection of lingerie, a purple see-through teddy that fastened down the front with tiny flowers. The cups were made of re-embroidered lace flowers and the straps were thin ribbons. There was a small ruffle around the bottom and she looked sexy and adorable at the same time.

"Thank you again for this, Philippe. I do have a weakness for pretty lingerie."

"No thanks are necessary, Cerise. If I'm going to be totally truthful it was more for me than for you. You look so hot," he said.

"I do, don't I?" Chastain continued to model for him. She finished by showing him her perfect behind and then doing the booty dance. "You have very good taste, *cher.* It's perfect. The suite is perfect and you," she said as she walked toward him, "aren't too bad, either."

He got up from his comfortable position on the floor and met her halfway.

"I can see I have more work to do," he said before swooping her up in his arms. She was giggling madly and Lulu hopped up and ran over to see what was going on.

"Now see what you did?" he said sternly.

"Oh, don't worry. Watch this," Chastain said. "Lulu, it's bedtime for little girls."

Lulu looked as though she might ignore her, but she did an abrupt about face and walked over to her bed.

She picked up her toy, turned around three times and settled down with the toy as a pillow.

Philippe carried Chastain in the bedroom, muttering under his breath. "Well, damn, if it was that easy why did I have to beg her for five minutes to get in the durned thing?"

Chastain was still laughing when he deposited her on the bed. He took off the robe and slid in next to her. "So are you still going to spend Christmas with me?"

"Yes, I am. But I can't have you spending a year's salary on the W. Where are we going to be?"

"Let me worry about that. I have a plan. After your folks leave, you'll find out what I have in mind."

She curled up next to him and combed her fingers through the dense chest hairs she loved so much. "They'll be here next week," she said dreamily.

"It'll be good to see them. Who's coming, besides Miz Lucinda?"

"Toto and Toot, for sure. I don't know if Nathan and Lambert will make it this trip. Tippy always feels like somebody in the family has to be there to make sure the restaurant is safe. Toto's assistant manager will run the store and Toot has a couple of assistants to keep the show bar up and running." Tippy was her grandmother's family nickname, as were Toto and Toot. People outside the family always called them by their proper names.

"They're going to get a real kick out of seeing the exhibit. They're really proud of you, Cerise. What else are you going to do while they're here?"

"Toto and Toot just want to see Harlem, every square inch of it. They had good times here back in the day. We might go to a play, but they'll be happy going to the jazz clubs and they will love Sylvia's. Tippy wants to go to Food Network. She's fascinated by that channel and I got tickets to the *Rachel Ray* show. And she might want to go shopping."

Her fingers suddenly stopped moving and she sat up with a frantic look on her face.

"What is it, darling? What's the matter?"

"Holy Mother of God, Philippe. It just dawned on me that my grandmother is going to see those pictures and it'll take her about a nanosecond to figure out who the model was. Tippy is gonna see your naked ass on display in front of God and everybody."

Philippe let out a booming laugh that lasted until he got a cramp in his side but Chastain didn't see the humor at that particular moment.

Chapter 13

The next morning Chastain woke slowly and reached over to touch Philippe. They had been entwined all night and she craved his warmth. What she got was a handful of Lulu, who was staring at her with her "I'm hungry" look. "Where did you come from, sweetie? Where's your daddy?" Chastain asked sleepily.

Philippe came into the bedroom, fully dressed. He looked wonderful.

"I've been up for a while. I took Miss Tallulah for her morning walk and ordered breakfast. I'm running a bath for you because I think you're going to need a nice long soak. You're probably sore all over," Philippe said.

Chastain sat up and hastily rubbed at her eyes lest

there be something crusty and unattractive in the corners. She threw the sheet back and started to swing her legs out of the bed. "Don't be silly, Philippe, I'm just, *ohh!*" she gasped. There was a distinct tightness in her legs and arms; they'd done some world-class lovemaking for quite a long time last night. "Oh, my soul, what's wrong with me?"

"Nothing a bath and a long massage won't cure." He came over to pick her up but she refused.

"You can't be carrying me around like Lulu," she said irritably. "I'm not an invalid." She got out of the bed and winced as she tried to take a step. "This is so wrong," she moaned.

She truly was sore all over. She'd used muscles she didn't even know she had, but she was determined to gather the scraps of her dignity and get in the tub on her own. The second step was better, but the third one made her whimper.

"Quit being a martyr," Philippe grumbled and picked her up with one arm. He ushered her into the bathroom and into the tub. "You'll thank me later."

The hot water was just what she needed. Lulu stood on her hind legs to inspect the proceedings but Chastain was too familiar with her behavior. "*Cher,* will you take her out of here? She's jumped in the tub before. The last time was the day after I had paid good money to have her groomed and it was not a happy day for me."

"C'mon, shorty, let's go get a café au lait for your mommy. How does that sound? We'll let you relax, Cerise."

She did relax, luxuriating in the bubbles that smelled strongly of Shalimar. Chastain only liked classic perfumes like Magie Noire, Chanel No.5 and Shalimar. Her close association with her grandmother and the showgirls at Uncle Toot's bar had formed her tastes and she saw no reason to change. The modern fragrances all smelled alike to her. Besides, Philippe always loved the way she smelled.

Philippe. She might eventually come to regret the time they were spending together, but it wouldn't be for a long time. She hadn't felt so cherished, so adored since the first time they'd made love. He was a wonderful lover back then and he was even better now. He was gentle, fierce, rough and tender and he made her feel like a queen. No, not a queen, a goddess. If she never let another man touch her for the rest of her life it wouldn't matter because no one could make her feel the way he did.

She'd had other lovers, but they simply didn't compare. One was from her grad school days; he was a nice enough fellow but the heat just wasn't there. She'd dated an incredibly beautiful African guy while she was in Paris. He was attentive and kind and brilliant, but the lovemaking didn't get the job done. And poor François, an ardent Parisian who'd wined, dined and wooed her for the better part of a year. When it was time for intimacy it just wasn't the way she remembered. Her partners had all been thrilled with the sex, but it wasn't enough for her. Philippe had taught her true passion and she couldn't and wouldn't settle for less.

She'd begun to believe there was something wrong with her because she couldn't achieve the ultimate high that lovemaking was supposed to bring. That was a gift that only Philippe could give her and it was one she would treasure as long as she lived. Maybe she was just asking for more heartache, but right now she just didn't care. Mona was right: Christmas in New York was a heady, romantic time and she was going to enjoy every single minute of it. How she'd feel when New Year's came was another matter. New Year's signaled the end of the holidays and logically it would be the end of her tryst with Philippe. But she could think about it later, when the time came. Right now all she wanted to think about was the sweet, sexy man who was doing everything possible to make sure she was having a fabulous holiday. *Philippe.*

Her eyes were closed and she was drifting into sleep when Lulu barked in her ear. Her eyes popped open and there she was, wearing her most endearing expression, the happy smile that won hearts and earned treats from anyone who was nearby. "You're back. Were you a good girl?"

Philippe appeared in the doorway with an amazingly fluffy terrycloth W robe. "She was a holy terror. She barked at everyone she saw and tried to chase a squirrel, five pigeons and a cab. Breakfast will be here in five minutes so unless you plan to starve, it's time for you to exit the bath."

"Oh, okay. I do feel much better, *cher.* Thank you so much."

"If you thank me one more time I'm going to withhold sexual favors. You don't thank someone for l—oh, good, the food's here. I'm starving."

"I'm coming, I'm coming!" She got out of the tub, patted herself dry and put on the robe.

The plan was for them to do some Christmas shopping and some serious touristy sightseeing, but Philippe vetoed the idea. "You need a nice long massage. Besides, it's snowing out there."

"Sounds like a plan. Do I go to the spa for this massage?"

They were finishing breakfast, which consisted of Chastain's favorite, blueberry pancakes. There was also turkey sausage and bacon, scrambled eggs, grits and Ruby Red grapefruit. She drank some of the excellent Jamaican coffee and made a sound of contentment.

"The food here is amazing, Philippe. Who knew they would have grits in a place like this?"

"Actually, Pop stayed here when he was courting Mom," Philippe said. "They met here in New York one weekend and it was the beginning of their romance. They both spoke so highly of the service here I thought it would be the perfect place for us."

His father, Mac, had been a widower for years before meeting and marrying his wife, Ruth. They had been married in Atlanta right after Hurricane Katrina and had been blissfully happy ever since.

Chastain looked under the table where Lulu was patting her leg. "No more treats for you, little girl.

You're going to get very chubby if I keep handing you tidbits every time you want one."

Without hesitation Lulu turned to Philippe but this time she stood up and put both forepaws on his knee. "Aww, Cerise, just one little bite. Look at her, she looks so sad."

"She's perfected that look over the years. Go ahead, be a patsy, see if I care. But just give her little bitty pieces about the size of the nail on your pinky."

There was a brisk knock at the door of the suite and Philippe stopping giving into Lulu's demands long enough to answer it. She helped him in his task by racing to the door barking her head off. He opened the door to admit a tall young man with a folded portable massage table and a handsome carrier for his creams, oils and towels.

"I'm Randall and I'm here for the massage," he said.

Philippe looked first at the young man with gleaming green eyes and then at Chastain. Randall was a real cutie with dark brown skin, a shaved head, neatly trimmed goatee and huge biceps. Lulu looked, too, but she seemed to like what she saw, unlike Philippe, whose thick brows were going lower and lower.

"Just leave the table. I'll call when it's time for you to pick it up."

"Oh, no, sir, I'm here to give the massage. Would you like the table in here or the bedroom?"

"The table can be set up in the second bedroom and then you can leave," Philippe said in a deceptively calm voice.

"But I give the massage," Randall said with confusion in his long-lashed eyes.

"Not today." Philippe didn't look pleasant in the least; he looked positively menacing as he stared at the confused young man. Lulu gave him her own stern look as well as a little growl. If Philippe didn't like the strange man, that was good enough for her.

Chastain had to cover her mouth to stifle her laughter. "It's okay, Randall. It's not you, it's them," she assured him. "Philippe, stop looming over the poor man and show him where you want the thing to go."

Philippe grudgingly showed him where to set up and seconds later Randall was practically sprinting out the door with Lulu nipping at his heels. When the door closed she gave a satisfied little "hmmf'" and went in search of her stuffed duck toy.

This time Chastain didn't hold back, she burst into peals of laughter. "You probably scarred him for life. He may never be the same."

"He'll get over it. I gave him a hundred-dollar tip."

"So why didn't you let him do the treatment? It actually would have cost less than the tip," she pointed out.

Philippe reached over and appropriated a segment of grapefruit that Chastain was about to eat. "In what universe do you think it would be okay for another man to put his hands on your body? You know it's not happening here on Earth, so where do you think it would be okay?"

"I think you're a little jealous, Philippe."

"Have we just met? Name one Deveraux man who'd let his wife get a massage at the hands of some random masseuse," he challenged.

"Have you forgotten that we're not married?" Chastain's voice sounded a little tight, but Philippe didn't notice.

"According to Jennifer, Jacques, Paul and Dominic we are. So no touchy-touchy by young Randall or anybody else. Your table awaits, Cerise."

Philippe certainly knew what he was doing when it came to massage. Raphael Saadiq's CD was playing and the music was as soothing to Chastain as the delicate scent of the warm oil he was using to relax her overworked muscles. She was on her stomach, her face in the padded hole at the head of the table and Philippe's very talented hands were making her melt.

"I would say that you're next, but I'm afraid I'm going to go right to sleep after this."

"That's the general idea, Cerise. No one said anything about quid pro quo. This all about you right now."

"I still can't believe you were jealous," she teased gently.

"Jealous, territorial, Type-A alpha male, call it whatever you want." He was working the kinks out of her lower back and behind with slow, deliberate movements. "Do you really think I'd let another man touch you like this?"

"Mmm," she said sleepily.

"It's not my most attractive characteristic, I'll grant

you that. But it's a human flaw we all share. Have you ever been bent out of shape over me?"

"Oh, hell yes," she said. "Every time I saw some baby-faced-D-cup-wearing-big-booty-having chocolate Amazon giving you face time I was livid. I thought you were having an affair with Ricki the first time I met her."

Philippe laughed, as his hands kept moving. "For God's sake, why would you think that?"

"First of all, you told me you had a date at the opening, remember? And I saw you leave with her. And second, once I saw Demetria's face I knew she was a Deveraux. I had a full minute of being really uncomfortable until Ricki told me about her other children and her husband. I was relieved to hear it because my blood had been boiling," she confessed.

Philippe was still laughing. "Chocolate Amazons? That's a new one."

"Oh, come on, Philippe. You Deverauxes have the same taste in women. Look at Maya and Nicole," she argued, refering to his sisters-in-law, both dark-skinned beauties with curves.

"And you look at Mom," he returned. "My father is the prototype of a true Deveraux man and Ruth doesn't fit your mold." It was true, his mother-by-marriage, as the brothers referred to her, was caramel-skinned with a perfect figure. "Quiet as it's kept, I'm allowed to form my own tastes and opinions, Cerise. I thought you knew that about me."

Chastain sighed with pleasure as he continued his

massage, working his way down her thigh. "You're right, Philippe. You were certainly the most iconoclastic member of your family. You were always your own man and went your own way. How could I have thought otherwise?" she mumbled to herself.

"One of the follies of youth. You're forgiven for your rush to judgment."

"I'll make it up to you," she promised, just before drifting off to sleep.

He leaned down and planted a kiss on her behind. "Not required. No quid pro quo, my love," he said, but she didn't hear him.

Chapter 14

The weekend was so sublime Chastain didn't want it to end. They had finally emerged from their cocoon in the W on Sunday. They went back to the loft in the late afternoon. As Lulu ran around the living room like a miniature racehorse, Chastain suggested that Philippe stay for a while.

"I'll make something for dinner," she told him.

"I don't want you to go to any trouble."

"It's no trouble at all. We've got to eat, don't we? You have to let me do things for you once in a while. You can't be the only one doing the giving," she pointed out.

She put her hands on her hips and looked as if she were ready to debate the point with him for hours if that's what it took to get him to agree.

"You're not going to give up, are you?"

"Have you ever known me to?" she asked.

"Only on me, Cerise. Only on me."

She was stung to her heart by his words. She couldn't speak; her hand went to the little diamond circlet that she hadn't removed since she'd put it on again. Philippe cupped her face with both hands. "I'm going to take Lulu out. Be right back."

Chastain stood by the elevator looking as stricken as she felt. She went to the bedroom to take off her coat and hang it up, and then to the bathroom to wash her hands. Her reflection in the mirror showed her feelings. She wasn't good at keeping a poker face. He thought she'd given up on him and now she wondered if he was right. Had she just thrown in the towel instead of letting him know exactly how she felt? She turned off the lights and went back to the kitchen. Having to cook a meal was a good thing. It would keep her busy while she mulled things over.

Opening the refrigerator was the first step. There had to be something in there she could make quickly. "Peanut butter, cheese, eggs, shallots, radishes," she said, tapping her lower lip with her forefinger. "That'll make a really nasty omelet. What's in the freezer?"

She was so engrossed in her search she didn't hear the elevator. She closed the freezer door and screamed when she saw Philippe on the other side of the door. The frozen chicken in her hand crashed onto her foot and she screamed again.

"Did I scare you, Cerise?"

"What do you think?" She hopped around the counter on her uninjured foot and sat down on the nearest stool. She took off her soft leather ballet slipper and tried to flex her foot. She was shouting "Ouch!" and Lulu was licking the sole of her foot while Philippe went into action. After tossing his coat aside he sank down on his heels to examine her foot carefully.

"I don't think it's broken, but we should probably go to the emergency room anyway. You should have that x-rayed."

Chastain despised hospitals because she associated them with the deaths of her parents. She had no idea why she felt like that, seeing as how she had no memory of either parent, but she just did. "I just need RICE," she protested.

"Are you that hungry? I can get something to eat, babe, but we need to get your foot in order first."

She laughed through the pain, and not just because Lulu was still licking her foot. "RICE is an acronym. It stands for Rest, Ice, Compression and Elevation. I need to put ice on my foot and elevate it and then I need to put an ACE bandage on it. I'm sure it's not broken, it just hurts."

"Well, darlin' if that's what you need, that's what you shall have. I'm going to put you in that big chair and get you all situated. Do you have an ACE bandage?"

"No, but I have some silk stockings. I got them in Paris. I don't have a lot of first aid stuff, *cher.*"

Philippe picked her up like she weighed about five pounds and put her into a big rounded chair that would easily hold two adults, possibly three. Lulu joined her, stretching across her lap. "Do you have an ice bag?"

"No but I have ice and Ziploc bags. We'll have to improvise."

Philippe got her comfortably settled with her foot elevated on an ottoman and two pillows, with the makeshift ice pack on the sore spot, which was reddened and swelling.

"What were you going to do with that chicken anyway?"

"I was going to cook it. David has a convection oven that can go from frozen to perfectly done in less than an hour."

"Isn't he special," Philippe said under his breath. "I'm going to get us some dinner and get you a wrap for your foot. Where are your keys?"

It was pointless to argue with him, so she settled back in the chair and closed her eyes. He'd turned on the flat-screen television and made her a cup of herbal tea before he left, so she was quite comfortable. She and Lulu were asleep in minutes.

Chastain's eyes opened to an appetizing aroma. "Something smells really good. What is it?"

"You're awake. How does your foot feel?"

She wiggled her toes. "Cold. I'm taking this thing off."

"Let me do that. I got your bandage," Philippe said.

He sat down on the ottoman and put her foot in his lap. He handed Chastain a bag, which she looked into curiously. "My word, did you buy out the store?" He'd purchased two kinds of elastic wrap, an elastic splint, aspirin, a thermometer, a huge box of bandages, antiseptic ointment and cough syrup. "What is all this, *cher?*"

"You said you didn't have any first aid type things so I got you some. Come eat before it gets cold. I called Antoine and he sent some food over. I told him anything but chicken, since you'd been attacked by one."

"You're hilarious."

Chastain stood up slowly and Philippe came to help her. "Honey, I'm fine. I can walk over to the table by myself," she fussed. He had his way, though.

Antoine had sent over bouillabaisse, grilled salmon on a bed of julienned vegetables, a sweet potato tian and fresh bread. There was also a bottle of sparkling water, and an open-faced tarte of caramelized pears and pecans.

"This was very thoughtful of you, Philippe. And very nice of Antoine," she added. "My foot feels much better and I've had a wonderful meal with a wonderful man. I couldn't be any happier."

Just then the phone rang and he handed the cordless phone to her without a word. She didn't look at the caller ID, she just answered with her usual hello.

"Am I calling at a good time?"

It was David. His voice was possibly the last one she wanted to hear right about now. She kept the conversation short, but the gist of it was that he would be back tomorrow and he hoped they could have dinner.

"Sure, David, that would be nice," she said distractedly. They agreed on a time and ended the call.

Philippe was putting food in Lulu's dish while she talked and he looked deep in thought. She didn't have to wonder what was on his mind, because he told her.

"Cerise, I don't like the idea of you staying here, especially now. I don't think it's safe and I don't like the idea of you living in another man's house."

"David owns this place, he doesn't live here," she said.

"If his name is on the deed, it's his place and I don't like it. I don't know if it's jealousy or just me being old-school, I just don't like it. You're going to have to make other living arrangements."

Chastain stared at him to see if he was perhaps making a joke. If it was supposed to be a joke it wasn't funny. He didn't look like he was trying to be funny; on the contrary he looked totally serious.

"Philippe, you look like you mean that," she said.

"I do."

"David has been kind enough to let me stay here rent-free and you think I should go somewhere else because of some macho mindset of yours?" Her voice was full of frustration, as was the expression on her face.

"That's an extreme way of looking at it, Chastain. It's not just because Llewellyn owns this place, although that's a big part of it. I just don't like the idea of you in this loft by yourself. I don't care what you say. It's not a secure enough environment," he said in a maddeningly reasonable voice.

"I have a roommate, Philippe, or did you forget that?"

"Where is she right now?"

"Mona went to D.C. to visit her father. She'll be back in a couple of days."

"So in the meantime you're here by yourself. I rest my case."

"You have no case, Philippe. I'm not a child. I'm perfectly capable of taking care of myself. I lived in this very city for several years without getting mugged, molested or subjected to random mayhem. I lived in Europe for three years without incident but now all of a sudden you act like I'm too weak-minded to be out on my own. Thanks for the vote of confidence, I really appreciate it."

She pushed her chair back and was about to start clearing the table but Philippe stopped her.

"I'll do that. You need to sit down and put your foot up."

Chastain wanted very much to defy him, but it was a reasonable suggestion and the foot was throbbing a bit. There was no point in taking a stand on principle if it was going to cause her pain. She limped over to the big chair without his assistance and refused when he asked if she wanted another ice pack.

"I don't want ice. I want to understand you, Philippe. You've gotten it into your head that I shouldn't be staying here and you want me to go live somewhere else. You seem to forget how expensive real estate is in this city. And you act as though I can just go out tomorrow and find another place to live. Besides being very ungracious to David, who's been a wonderful host, it will be impossible to find someplace decent to live this close to the holidays."

"Those are all valid points, Cerise. Even the one about Llewellyn," he said grudgingly. "It was very nice of him to offer you a place to stay while you're here." His eyes grew thoughtful. "Are you planning on living here again?"

"What are you getting at, Philippe?"

"When you came back from France, what was your plan? Were your planning on staying in New York or moving back home or what?"

Chastain was mildly surprised by the question. "I don't know. I hadn't really finalized my plans. I was going to decide before the exhibit closed. I'm not planning on going back to Europe or anything, but I hadn't decided whether I was going back to New Orleans, either. New York is a good place for an artist," she said slowly.

"So is New Orleans," he countered. "That's one of the great things about being a creative force in the universe—you can do what you do wherever you are."

"What? What are you saying, Philippe?"

He eased himself down into the big plushy chair and pulled her into his lap. Lulu, who had been pacing around the living room with him, jumped up to join them. "What I'm saying is I have the perfect solution. Come live with me."

Chapter 15

Chastain clicked the remote control like an automaton. She wasn't watching anything; she was just surfing. Sitting in the big chair with her feet on the ottoman and Lulu in her lap, she was grimly inspecting every station and finding them all wanting. "There are like nine million channels out there and nothing I want to watch. Oh, look, Lulu, a dog show."

Mona took the remote and said, "Okay, leave it on the dog show. I'm taking this away so you don't sprain your thumb." She sat on the sofa and looked at her friend. "Are you going to tell me what I busted up when I got back last night?"

Chastain raised an eyebrow. "Only if you tell me

why you came back early. I thought you weren't getting back until Tuesday."

Mona groaned and stretched out on the sofa, staring up at the ceiling. "I came back because my father is a tyrant and a dictator and he wants to run my life."

"How so?"

"He has this embassy position lined up for me and he insists that I take it. I don't want to work at some freakin' embassy. I have no desire whatsoever to take that job. I'm not interested in policy, politics or politicians and working in an embassy is like a perfect storm of all those things with some boring protocols thrown in. It's not what I want to do."

"Mona, you love politics! You were glued to the TV during the presidential election and if you could get nothing but CNN on TV you'd be perfectly happy," Chastain reminded her.

"I will admit that President Obama may have excited my semi-dormant germ of political awareness, but not to the point where I want to take part in the boring, useless pompous end of the political process."

"Don't hold back, Monie. Tell me how you really feel," Chastain said dryly.

"My father is a bully, that's how I feel. We can't have a normal conversation about anything. He lays down the law and I break it. If he says one thing I'll say the other, just to get on his nerves. I don't even know why I do that, it's just like an automatic reaction," Mona admitted.

"Frustrating, isn't it?" Chastain said sympathetically.

"Do you get along with your dad?"

"I don't have one, Mona. My mother died when I was a baby, but my father died before I was born. That's why my grandmother and my great-uncles and uncles and aunts raised me. It took a big village to raise this wild child," she joked.

"I'm sorry, I didn't mean to say anything stupid, but when my mouth is open, my foot must go in it. Another reason I couldn't possible do anything with the diplomatic corps. Think what havoc I could wreak," she said with a groan.

"Honey, you don't owe me an apology. I had the most colorful childhood in the world and it made me the woman I am today. The cranky, mean, gimpy woman you see before you."

Mona turned on her side. "So how did you hurt your foot? After I broke up your tryst with Philippe you just went to bed and we never got a chance to dish. So what happened?"

"I dropped a frozen chicken on my foot. And what you broke up was about to be a fight. Philippe took me to the W hotel for the weekend and it was just amazing, Mona. One of the most wonderful weekends of my life, as a matter of fact."

"And? What happened to take you from weekend rapture to Sunday night fight?"

"Philippe has decided that he isn't comfortable with me living in David's house, as he puts it. I told him that David didn't live here, he just owns it, but Philippe's not having it. He just hates the idea of me being here."

"Well, you can't blame him for that, Chastain. He

may not live here, but if his name is on the place he owns it. What kind of man wants his woman living under another man's roof?"

Chastain gave Mona a look of horror. "That's exactly what Philippe said. Except for the part about me being his woman. We didn't get that personal. He just said he didn't like me being here and he wants me to move in with him."

"And that's a bad thing?" Mona asked.

"If he'd told me that he wanted me to live with him because he loved me and couldn't live without me, I would have felt better about it. That would have been kind of romantic in a way. But this 'come live with me' business, no. Unh-unh."

"So what did you say to him?"

"I was going to do quite a bit of yelling and screaming, but I didn't get around to it. He got in the chair with me and we started kissing and then you came in and the window of immediate opportunity closed. So he's got a verbal beat down coming from me," she said sternly.

"Time out, Chastain. You were going to stay with him for the holidays anyway, so why were you going to get all mean and evil about it? That doesn't make sense to me."

"Because staying with him for Christmas is one thing and moving in with him is something else. If he really cared about me he would be asking for something permanent," she said stubbornly.

Mona sat up and put her feet on the floor, leaning

forward to press her point. "Chastain, you know th man is crazy about you. I thought David had the hot for you but he's lukewarm compared to Philippe. He may not say it in words but his actions are speaking i you just listen. I saw Lulu's new bordello bed and the Tiffany doggie dishes. And think about how muc money you raised when he bought the triptych. He could have bought a small piece but he didn't hol back at all. That was a lot of money, Chastain."

Chastain's face paled and she put both her hands t her cheeks. "What did you say?"

"Why are you looking like that *Home Alone* kid? said he spent a lot of money buying the triptych," Mon said, clearly mystified.

"I never said thank-you," Chastain said bleakly. " always thank my patrons and send them a nice letter. did that with every single person who bought a paintin except Philippe. I never even said a word about it, lik it was just nothing. I'm such an idiot," she said.

Mona was impressed by the emotion she wa seeing. "So, whatcha gonna do?"

"I have no idea," Chastain said. "Just none. My folk will be here on Wednesday. I have to tell David that I'n blowing him off and I have to make a sincere and heart felt apology to Philippe. I don't think life can get any better, do you?"

"Yes, it can. Let me get that Ben & Jerry's out of the freezer and you'll see just how good life can be High-fat gourmet ice cream is just the thing to get you troubles in perspective," Mona said.

Chastain hoped she was right because right now the troubles were looming large.

David insisted that they stay in, once he saw her sprained foot. "You should have gone to the emergency room for that," he said. "I can take you right now."

"Oh, please no. I went through all of that with Philippe last night. I'm fine, really. I lazed around all day and now I'm fine."

"Deveraux was here when you were injured?"

Chastain raised an eyebrow. David's voice had an odd edge to it, although it really wasn't so odd when given his feelings. "Yes, David. Philippe and I spent the weekend together." She waited for his reaction.

He gave her a rueful smile. "I've really got to work on my timing," he said. "I should have made a move on you years ago. When you were my student you were off-limits, but after that, I should have put all my cards on the table. Instead I hesitated and I lost."

"David, I never knew you felt like that," Chastain said. "You were always so casual and you treated me like a pal, a buddy. I'm not good at reading between the lines, I guess."

"You were dating someone when you got out of my class. Then when you were free I was involved with someone. When I was in Paris I thought we might have a chance because you were unattached. I should have been more direct about my intentions instead of trying to be suave," he said with a smile.

Chastain shook her head. "David, I don't think it would have done any good. Whether I like it or not, Philippe is in my blood. You could have swept me off my feet with carriage rides and aisle seats to the best plays and anything else you could think of but the end results would be the same," she said. "You're a great guy and any sane woman would be glad to have your interest but I'm afraid that I'm fated to be a fool for him for the rest of my life."

She looked so forlorn that David put his arm around her shoulders and gave her a one-armed hug. "Don't knock it, honey. A lot of people go through life wishing they had that kind of grand passion."

"Have you had one David?"

He nodded. "I thought I had. I dated a woman for years. She was my high school sweetheart, then my college sweetheart, then we had an argument and she married someone else. I hated her for a long time because she waited until the week before the wedding to break it off with me," he said. "But anyone capable of exciting great love can do the opposite. That's what makes it passion, I guess."

"Maybe that explains it because I was on the verge of breaking that vase over Philippe's head last night," she said grumpily.

"Which one, the blue one or the green?"

"The blue one."

David pretended to blow out a huge sigh of relief. "Thank God it was the blue one. The green one cost about two thousand dollars. The blue one came from

T.J. Maxx on clearance." They were laughing when Mona emerged from the bedroom.

"I'm going to Sylvia's for takeout. Can I bring you anything?"

David stood up and said he had a better idea. "You ladies call in the order and I'll go get it. Put the order under my name," he added, as he got ready to leave.

"That's a really nice guy. He's going to make someone a wonderful husband one day," Mona said.

"Yes, he will. I wish I was smart enough to be that woman," Chastain replied.

"You'd be safe but you wouldn't be fulfilled. You belong to Philippe and he belongs to you. Period. The sooner you get your little ducks in a row the happier you'll be."

"You make it sound so easy," Chastain said in a voice that was dangerously close to a whine.

"It's as easy as you want it to be or as hard as you make it. So whatcha gonna do?"

Chastain groaned and patted her lap so Lulu would jump up. "I have no idea, Mona. Just none. Philippe is going to Washington tonight and he'll be there for a couple of days. I hope I can figure something out by the time he gets back because he's expecting an answer."

Mona gave her a sympathetic look. "Just say yes," she advised.

"You make it sound so easy," Chastain repeated irritably.

"It is, my sister. Just follow your heart and say yes."

Chapter 16

Two days later Chastain was about to leave the studio to head for the airport when she got a surprise. Ricki had surprised her by showing up at Studio L in a long black car with a handsome driver.

"We don't use the town car that much. It needs to get out," she said. "I actually think we're going to sell it. It makes more sense to rent one for the times when we really need one."

It was a long explanation for a simple favor, but Chastain wasn't going to question it. She did have another question for her, though. "How did you know they were coming in today?"

"Philippe said something about it," Ricki answered airily, as if it were of no importance at all.

"By the way, Antoine would like you to be his guests tonight."

"At Zazu's? That's wonderful, Ricki, but it's too much."

"Don't be silly. He's looking forward to entertaining you. And it's going to be at a different restaurant. This one is called Lagniappe. It's his pet because it's the first restaurant he opened. That place is his baby," she said.

"Ricki, that's so sweet of him. They'll really enjoy it, especially my grandmother. You're just too thoughtful," she said.

"Don't mention it. We'll just drop me off at home and then you're off to the airport."

Chastain stopped to talk to Veronica, who was standing by her desk looked especially attractive in a leopard print silk blouse and a black pencil skirt. "Veronica, I'll be back in an hour or so, I guess." She glanced at the fabulous black stilettos the other woman was wearing and grinned. "Can you run in those things?"

Veronica looked startled, but said, "I could if I had to, I suppose. Why do you ask?"

"Because my uncles are gonna be on you like a duck on a junebug. They love pretty women and they really don't believe they're a day over forty, so be prepared. When you see two identical white-haired gentlemen come in here with Cazal tinted glasses on, *duck*." She laughed.

"Oh, girl, I thought you were serious! I'm sure

they're just sweet Southern gentlemen," Veronica said
with a smile.

"Don't say I didn't warn you."

A few hours later, Veronica had a flattered but wary
expression on her face. She was sitting on a banquette
with two very handsome men, one on either side.
Theotis, known to family as Toto, and Thaddeus,
known as Toot, were admiring her bounty with no
shame in their game. They were twins, about six feet
tall with wavy silver hair and unlined caramel skin. It
was hard to believe that they were over sixty years old.

"You should come back to N'Awlins with us,
darlin'. The cold weather up here doesn't suit you."
Toto gave her a smile that could melt a glacier. She
giggled like a schoolgirl.

"He's right, sweetheart. You need to be where the
weather is warm and the men are hot. The Big Easy is
just the place for you," Toot said smoothly. More
giggles ensued. It would have gone on for some time,
but Chastain intervened.

"Uncle Theotis and Uncle Thaddeus, you're scaring
this poor woman. She's not used to the Thibodaux
charm. Let her get back to work and you two come look
at the rest of the exhibit," she said.

"Baby, your artwork is wonderful. We're very proud
of you. But this young lady is a work of art," Toot said.
"How can we not admire her, too?"

"Besides," Toto said with a wicked grin, "we've
seen naked men before."

"That was a low blow, Toto. I'ma get you for that," she said.

She'd been on edge all the way from the airport because she knew that the nudes were practically the first thing anyone saw when they walked into the gallery. That was what she wanted because the pictures were like a declaration of self for Chastain. However, they took on a whole new perspective when her grandmother was the audience. Chastain had braced herself for the worst possible reaction to the life-size salutes to the male anatomy, but Lucinda Thibodaux had shocked the life out of her.

She'd no sooner relinquished her coat to the attentive studio manager, James, than her eyes went directly to the dreaded trio. Lucinda had walked right over to them, whipping out her glasses as she did so. "My, my, my, Chastain," she said, linking her arm with her granddaughter's. "These are magnificent. You have a real gift, my dear." She nudged her affectionately and added, "And excellent taste in subject matter."

And that was all she had to say on the matter. They continued to walk through the exhibit and Lucinda gave every indication that she was enjoying herself thoroughly. She was particularly taken with a group of pastels that depicted Chastain's life in the French Quarter. There was Lucinda cooking, Lucinda regaling a guest with some story, Toto and Toot playing with their zydeco band, and others. Chastain was amazed to see tears in her grandmother's eyes. Lucinda was such a pragmatist, so grounded, it wasn't like her to show this much emotion.

"Tippy, are you getting tired? We can go upstairs and you can relax and have a cup of coffee. Chock full o' Nuts with chicory, just the way you like it," Chastain said. "I don't want you to be too tired. We're going to a special restaurant for dinner."

"That's a good idea, honey. I could use a cup of coffee and I want to see that little strumpet of yours. Is she still a scandal?"

Chastain laughed as they headed to the elevator. "I think she's gotten worse, Tippy. Every man she meets is fair game to her."

"Good for her, the little strumpet. Where is she?"

The elevator stopped on three and they stepped into the living room. "She's in her crate in my bedroom. Let me go get her and you get comfortable."

Lulu came out of the bedroom at breakneck speed because she knew an old friend was there. She was particularly fond of Lucinda because she always gave her good things to eat and she knew how to scratch her ears the way she liked.

"There's my little girl," Lucinda said warmly. Lulu was in her lap, trying to lick her chin and Lucinda was laughing at her. "I don't know why you keep her in that awful crate, Chastain. She's a good little girl, aren't you, sweetie?"

"It's because she has separation anxiety when I'm away. If I put her in the crate she feels safe and she knows I'll be back soon," Chastain explained. "And she's not as good as you might think," she added dryly. "She has a sick attraction to toilet paper, paper towels and books. She's better than a paper shredder."

She went into the kitchen to make the coffee. While she was getting out cups and saucers, she had a chance to take a good look at her beloved grandmother. Tippy was still gorgeous at sixty-seven. Her caramel skin didn't have a line in it, her figure was still tight and firm, and if it weren't for the fact that she had hair so white it shone like platinum, she could easily pass for a woman in her forties. She was only five foot four, but she carried herself as if she was much taller. Stylish, outspoken and full of humor, Lucinda Thibodaux was one hell of a woman.

She gradually urged Lulu off her lap and stood up, brushing imaginary hairs off her lap. "Where is the bathroom, *cherie?* I need to wash up a bit."

Chastain showed her around the loft, ending in the bathroom. "Very fancy. This David Llewllyn is certainly making every effort to impress you. He must be in love," she said.

"Um, well, he says he's quite fond of me," Chastain demurred.

"I figured as much. Let me freshen up and I'll be right out."

Chastain stared at the door her grandmother just closed in her face. *The woman is part witch,* she thought. She always had a way of getting right down to the basics of any situation.

When Tippy came out of the bathroom, Chastain

had set a place for her at bar of the work island. In addition to the coffee, there was a bowl with a sectioned Ruby Red grapefruit, kiwi and starfuit. She'd also put out croissants, small cheese danish and the bacon was in the oven. Tippy had taught her how to cook when she was a child and cooking bacon in the oven ensured that it was evenly browned, crisp and not nearly as greasy as the pan fried variety.

"This is so nice, *cherie*. The coffee smells good. There's nothing like the smells of coffee and bacon in the morning," Lucinda said as she seated herself at the bar. "Will you stop fiddling around over there and come talk to me, child? I haven't seen you in a year," she said, patting the stool next to her.

Chastain put the bacon on a plate and joined her, giving her another big hug and kiss on the cheek before she sat down. "You look fabulous, Tippy. How do you do it?"

"I eat well, I sleep eight hours a night and I do my yoga and Pilates every day. And I pray every day, as I hope you're doing, too. I enjoy every day of my life, that's how I do it. But I don't want to talk about me, let's talk about you. You look very well and satisfied. Does Philippe Deveraux have anything to do with the glow in your cheeks?"

Chastain was about to take a bite of a piece of bacon but her grandmother's words made her drop it on the floor. Lulu happily pounced on it, chewing it in dainty little bites.

"What do you mean, Tippy? What makes you think

he has anything to do with, well, anything?" she asked in a faint voice.

"Child, please. You act like I don't know you, like I didn't raise you from a baby. I know that Philippe is in New York and I know it didn't take him but a hot minute to get to you. He's always been in love with you and once you were back from France I'm sure he didn't waste any time in winning you back." She drank coffee and made a satisfied face. "Very good, Chastain. You haven't lost your touch."

Chastain could feel a red-hot flush working its way up her neck. "Tippy, what in the world do you mean he's always been in love with me? You were the one who always said he was all wrong for me. You couldn't stand him and you didn't want him anywhere around me," she reminded her.

Tippy finished off a bite of her danish with another bracing sip of coffee, waving her hand airily as she did so. "That was so long ago. I didn't dislike Philippe. I just didn't want you following the same road that I walked, that your mother walked. You were too young to be so caught up with a man and that's why I told him he had to leave you alone. He did as I asked and look how well everything turned out."

"You did what?" Chastain sounded incredulous because she was. She couldn't believe what she was hearing.

"When you were in your last year of high school I knew all about you and young Deveraux and I asked him to meet with me. I told him that you were too young and naive to be so deeply involved with a young man. He had traveled all over with his family, he grew up with money and privilege and he was in a position to do anything he wanted with his life," she said passionately.

She wiped her hands on a cloth napkin before taking both of Chastain's hands. "You were too young, sweetheart. You had never been outside Louisiana, never been with another man, you had your whole life ahead of you. I didn't want you to end up like me and your mother. We made terrible mistakes and I could see you about to do the same."

Chastain tried to pull her hands away, but Tippy was too strong and too quick. She continued to hold on to her while she talked. "When I was sixteen years old, I got all caught up with the son of a rich man. When I got pregnant with your mother, he acted as if he'd never heard of me. I was left to raise my child alone, without help. My father turned me out and the only contact I had with my family was my brothers. If it hadn't been for Thaddeus and Theotis, I wouldn't have had any family at all. Eventually, after your mother, Cecelia, was born, they took me back, but it was never the same," she said sadly.

Fascinated in spite of herself, Chastain had questions. "Tippy, why didn't you ever tell me this before?" Chastain's eyes were large and teary. "What does this have to do with my mother? What happened with her?"

Tippy released one of Chastain's hands so she could drink more coffee. "You're a lot like Cecelia," she said reflectively. "She was so pretty, so full of life. She was a very talented young woman, too. You get your artistic talent from her. When she was seventeen, just graduated from high school and on her way to college, Cecelia got pregnant. Some high-toned triflin' son of a very wealthy family," she said with disgust. "When she told him she was carrying his child, he disappeared. His family sent him to California to go to college and that was that. Cecelia was heartbroken. She tried to find out where he was and she must have done so because she disappeared. We were all frantic, looking for her everywhere. I thought I would lose my mind trying to find my pregnant daughter who was out of her mind with grief."

She let go of Chastain's hand so she could dab her eyes with a napkin. "She finally came back with you in her arms. You weren't even a month old. She only stayed a few days," Tippy said. "One morning I got up because you were crying and I went in her bedroom and she was gone. She'd gotten up in the middle of the night and left."

"She left me?"

"Yes, *cher,* she did. I've never regretted being the one to raise you. You were a beautiful sweet little baby and you were always my joy—our joy, because everyone in the family loved you to pieces," she said, stroking Chastain's cheek.

Chastain's head was reeling by now. "So because you were a teenage mother and my mother was the same, you just automatically assumed that I was headed for the same fate and you warned off Philippe. Who jumped right through your hoop like a trained dog and dumped me. Is that what I'm to understand?"

Tippy calmly got up and poured more coffee. "That's about it in a nutshell. Except for the part about Philippe being a trained dog. That's unfair to him, Chastain. That boy really cared about you and he simply saw reason, that's all. He didn't want to do it, but I convinced him that it was the best thing for you. He did it out of love, *cherie*. After you graduated from college I thought you would find your way back to him but you were off again to New York, which caused him a great deal of pain. I could see it in his eyes whenever I saw him. Then I thought you were back together for sure after Katrina, but you ran out on him again, to France of all places." She gave Chastain a disapproving look.

"Now that you're back together don't do anything else to the poor man or you might lose him forever. He loves you but you test him, Chastain. A man can only take so much."

Chastain was dumbfounded. She was fingering her earring while Lulu was patting her leg for more bacon and her grandmother sat eating fruit as if nothing had happened. Tippy looked up to see the expression on her face and had the nerve to smile.

"What's the matter, baby girl? Cat got your tongue?"

Chapter 17

Chastain couldn't believe the older woman's casual attitude. "No, the cat doesn't have my tongue, but you're gonna wish it did," she said. She didn't bother to disguise the anger she was feeling. It rolled right out of her. "How can you sit there like nothing's wrong after the load of crap you just dumped on me?"

"I can do it because nothing is wrong. I told you some family truths that you're old enough to know about. I also told you the truth about Philippe. You think I was overstepping my boundaries when I sent him packing but you weren't raising you. I was raising you and I did what I thought was best. In the end it really didn't have any effect on you, did it? You've got your education, you've been able to travel and see the world and you're getting recognition for your work. Would any of that have happened if you stayed in New Orleans and hung on his every word?"

She answered her own question with a shrug. "Maybe it would have, but most likely it wouldn't have. Now you're good and grown and so is he and you still have passion for one another. Now is the right time to be with him and you are, so what's the problem?"

"How did you even know he was in New York?" Chastain snapped. "Have you been keeping tabs on me all this time?"

"You sound a little paranoid, sweetie. I knew he was here because Paris told me when she was in town visiting her people," she said. "Stop looking at me like I committed a crime."

"So that story you told me about my father dying, that was a lie, wasn't it?"

A lesser woman would have cowered under Chastain's scornful expression, but that woman wasn't Lucinda Thibodaux. "I said he died before you were born and when he left my daughter he was dead to me, so it wasn't a lie from my point of view."

"I don't believe this," Chastain said, shaking her head. "If someone had told me you could be this manipulative and selfish I wouldn't have believed a word of it and I would have been dead wrong. How could you do this to me?"

"How could I raise you with love and understanding? How could I give you the independence to pursue your dreams? Is that what you're so upset about Chastain? Because if it is you need to turn the heat down to a simmer, *cher.* What do you think would have happened if you had stayed in New Orleans and kept sneaking around with Philippe?"

"We'll never know, will we? For all you know it could have worked out perfectly," Chastain interrupted.

"Yes, and I could be Marie LeVeq returned from the grave, but I'm not. I live in the real world, baby girl. I had to deal with the thought that you could have gotten pregnant, which was a very good possibility," she pointed out. "I knew the very day you started having sex with that boy and it was just dumb luck that you didn't make a baby. It's all water under the bridge now so there's no need to get all melodramatic. You and Philippe still care about each other and you've got the rest of your lives to be together, so what's the problem? What's that they say? 'No harm, no foul'." She calmly took another section of grapefruit and made a sound of satisfaction. "This was delicious, sweetheart. I want to take a shower and change clothes. I plan to do some sightseeing while I'm here."

"I plan to divorce my whole family while you're here," Chastain retorted. "You are the very limit, Tippy. No wonder you're not married, you would have driven a man absolutely crazy." She picked up a piece of bacon and automatically broke off a piece for Lulu before remembering that she'd already had more than her fair share.

"Tell me something, Tippy. I have to ask because

there were obviously a lot of holes in the family history I was given before today. Is my mother really dead or did you make that up, too?"

Tippy froze with a spoon halfway to her mouth. This was something to which she didn't have a glib answer. The spoon went back into the bowl of fruit and she picked up her napkin to dab at her mouth. "As far as I know she's dead. I never laid eyes on her again and I haven't heard a word from her, either. We hired a detective and everything, but we never turned up anything. So that part, I believe, is true," she said in a soft, sad voice.

Chastain reacted by standing up and putting her arms around her grandmother. She held her tightly and pressed her cheek to her hair. "You are a hot mess, Tippy, but you're my hot mess. You were better to me than most mothers and I had a ball growing up with you. Even if you did mess with my head and Philippe's head and get all up in my business," she said with a shaky laugh.

Tippy's spunk came back quickly. "Sweet girl, you weren't supposed to be having any business at your age. You were barely sixteen when you and Philippe were carrying on. I should have never let those nuns promote you two grades. Your little fast tail could have gotten in a pile of trouble with him. As nice as his daddy is, I don't think he would have wanted a grandchild. And what would it have done to your friendship with Paris?"

Chastain smoothed Tippy's thick, gleaming hair. "We need to leave this topic of conversation alone for now because I'm still processing it. I do have one more question for you. Who is my father?"

Tippy got off lightly because Mona made one of her timely entrances right after Chastain asked her question. Chastain was perfectly willing to bide her time because she was going to get some answers out of Tippy before she went back to Louisiana. She could be just a stubborn as her grandmother when she needed to be. She introduced Mona to Tippy and got busy clearing up the kitchen while she thought about what she'd learned. *Philippe let me go so I could grow up. He did that for me, for us, because he wanted to have a future with me,* she thought. *Or maybe I'm romanticizing things again.*

She decided to stop overthinking and stay focused on one thing at a time. The only person she needed to be talking to was Philippe and he was still in D.C. In the meantime, she needed to take her great-uncles to the hotel where they insisted on staying. Mona had offered to stay with her sorority sister so they could have her room, but Chastain told her it wasn't necessary.

"They have their hearts set on staying at the Trump. These are some big ballers you're talking about. They want to come and go as they please and they'll probably meet some willing women while they're here, so it's best for all of us if they have their own accommodations."

Her grandmother would be staying at the loft,

though, and Chastain planned on grilling her until the wee small hours of the morning. In the meantime, once Tippy had showered and changed into a sophisticated black pantsuit with a violet silk sweater under it, they went out. They still had the use of the town car, so they took the uncles to the Trump Towers. They swaggered in looking like the men of the world they were, and Chastain had to laugh in delight at their enjoyment of their entrance.

After window shopping and seeing a few sights, they decided to go back to Studio L to get ready for dinner. David was there and Chastain introduced him to Tippy.

"My, you're handsome," she said in her frank, disarming way. "You've been a good friend to my granddaughter and I appreciate all the kindness you've shown her."

David reacted to her charming manner the way all men did. He bowed over her hand and kissed it, while assuring her that no thanks were necessary. "It's been my pleasure, Ms. Thibodaux. Chastain has always been a very special person to me and her talent makes my gallery look good. I'm looking forward to tomorrow night and I hope you are, too."

The next night would be a silent auction for charity. There would be a New Orleans style zydeco band and Creole and Cajun food in honor of Chastain's family heritage. David had gone to a lot of trouble to get it all set up and Chastain had just a shimmer of guilt about it. She knew his efforts partially stemmed from his unrequited feelings for her and she felt badly. Tippy had no qualms, however, and told him how much she was looking forward to the evening.

Soon it was time to get ready to go to Lagniappe for dinner. Tippy had a pretty navy blue jersey dress to wear that showed off her figure and her legs. She was going to wear pumps with the outfit but Chastain suggested she borrow a pair of knee-high boots.

"You're not used to the cold. I'm not sending you home with the flu or something. You need to bundle up a little," she cautioned her.

"As long as I'll look good I'll wear them. I don't mind being a little cold, you know. Beauty has no pain, baby girl. I've been telling you that for years. What are you wearing?"

"A brown pantsuit," Chastain said. She laughed at the look on Tippy's face.

"That sounds so drab," she said. "I don't want to see you looking dowdy. Wear a dress."

Chastain laughed again and put the suit on. It had high-waisted pants that fit perfectly and a bolero jacket that flared out at the bottom and had a collar that stood up. She wore a camisole with it that was the same rich sherry color as her eyes and was made of heavy silk re-embroidered lace. The total effect was feminine, fresh and daring. The only jewelry she wore, other than the diamond necklace, was a big costume brooch set with flame, gold and orange rhinestones. Her eyes were cleverly shadowed with bronze and gold and she had gold lip gloss over her ruby lipstick.

"Am I too drab now, Tippy?"

"Girl, you look like me in my heyday. It's too bad Philippe is out of town," Tippy mused.

Mona complimented both ladies as they emerged from the bedroom. "You're breathtaking. We've got to take pictures tonight."

"You're looking quite spectacular yourself. You should be going out dancing instead of to a family dinner," Chastain told her.

Mona was wearing a deep red dress that fit like a coat of paint. It had a high neck and deeply cut armholes but she had chosen to wear a cardigan in the same color so she was more covered up. The red color was fantastic with her rich chestnut skin and her black hair was a mass of thick curls. With lots of black mascara and a shiny red gloss on her lips, she looked hot.

"Tina, my sorority sister, wants to go to Tenjune later so I will be doing some dancing tonight, at least I hope so."

Tippy nodded and said, "Just take the little sweater off when you get to the club, honey. You'll be beating the men off with a stick."

They all laughed as they prepared to leave. Lulu looked doleful but brightened up after Chastain showed her a handful of Pup-peroni. She ran to her crate and waited patiently.

"I still don't like to see her in that thing," fussed Tippy. "She's the only great-grandchild I've got and you've got her caged up like a dog," she sniffed.

Chastain had her mouth open to remind her that Lulu was a dog and then she gave up. "Let's go. I can't be the only one who's hungry and we have to pick up the uncles."

Chastain had been absolutely correct when she thought that Tippy and Antoine would enjoy each other. Tippy was at her flirtatious best and Antoine thought she was absolutely captivating. He insisted on giving her a tour of his kitchen and they made a date to cook together before she went home to New Orleans. Ricki was amused to no end.

"Your family is wonderful, Chastain. Your uncles are something else."

"Just be careful around them or they'll try to carry you back home with them," she replied. "They're very impressed with you."

"That's sweet. Me, an old married lady with five boisterous children," she laughed.

"Why didn't you bring them tonight? They're very well-behaved, despite what you and Antoine say," Chastain told her.

"It's a school night and I like them to get in bed early. Plus, it's nice to have adult conversation for a change," she admitted cheerfully.

They were in a private dining room that was decorated in browns, golds and coppers, like the rest of the restaurant. Langniappe was very different from Zazu's, not just in appearance but in cuisine. The food was heartier, more like upscale peasant fare than the more modern cuisine at the other restaurant. Everything was delicious and everyone praised the food and the wine with great enthusiasm. Chastain looked at Tippy quizzically.

"Since you're in a truth-telling mood, is that thing about alcoholism in our family true?"

"Not that I know of. I just didn't want you to drink so I made up a little story," she said guilelessly.

"You have no shame whatsoever, do you? Have you ever told me the truth about anything?" Chastain was exasperated now. There was no point in being angry.

Tippy raised her glass of wine and gave her an unrepentant grin. "I didn't lie about how he feels about you," she said as she inclined her head toward the doorway.

Chastain looked up to see Philippe entering the room and she rose from the table. Without thinking about what she was doing she went to him and before she knew it, his arm was around her waist and he was bending his head to hear what she was saying.

"Philippe, I need to talk to you. Can we go somewhere private, please?"

"If that's what you want, of course we can. Let me say hello to everyone first, if that's all right with you," he said.

They went around the table with their hands entwined so he could say hello to everyone. Her uncles greeted him warmly and Tippy gave him a big hug and kiss on the cheek. If he was surprised by her show of affection, he didn't show it. Chastain wanted to leave as soon as possible, but Philippe was determined to act like a civilized adult. Finally she whispered to him that they had to leave right now or she wouldn't be responsible for her subsequent actions.

"You must really have something on your mind. Okay, Cerise, let's go."

Toot looked at the departing couple and said, "That's the last we'll see of them tonight."

Chapter 18

Philippe hailed a cab and they got in. He gave the driver an address but Chastain wasn't listening to him. She was still holding his hand as though it were her life preserver in a stormy sea. She was uncharacteristically quiet, which gave him more than a little concern.

"Cerise, what's the matter, angel? You seem upset about something."

"I'm not upset," she said. "I just missed you and I need to talk to you. And I need this," she added, pulling his head down to hers for a kiss.

He didn't know why she was being so affectionate, but he wasn't going to question it. He'd missed her, too, and her luscious lips were just what he wanted to taste.

"I hope that lipstick is the kind that doesn't come off because I'll be wearing it," he said

"Let's put it to the test." She smiled for the first time and the low sexy giggle he loved bubbled out of her throat.

All too soon the cab arrived at a beautifully restored brownstone in a residential area not too far from Zazu's. Chastain was looking around, mystified. "Philippe, where are we?"

"You'll find out in a minute. Come on in," he invited.

He opened the front door and they were in the foyer of what looked like a really nice home.

"Whose house is this?" she asked.

"This place belongs to Antoine, sort of. You know he's got a program to teach the restaurant business to displaced people, right? Well, the Food Network wants to do a reality show about it. Antoine agreed as long as it wasn't some kind of competition. He wants to house them here while the show is going on. Since it won't start until February, he'd offered me the use of the place until then. It's not completely furnished, but come and take a look," he said.

They walked down the hall into the living room, which was completely outfitted, right down to a Christmas tree. Chastain covered her mouth with her hand and stared.

The tree was a live one, about four feet tall and it was potted so it could be replanted. It wasn't decorated yet, but the room was heady with the scent of pine.

There was a comfortable set of couches, and a couple of chairs, which flanked the fireplace and two ottomans. The coffee table was long and wide and it was upholstered so it could double as seating. The color scheme was mostly neutral taupe with touches of ivory and beige, but some colorful paintings, pillows and rugs would remedy that. The dining room had a long table with no chairs, but the kitchen was set up for budding chefs with every appliance, dish and utensil imaginable.

On the second floor there were four bedrooms, the largest of which was completely done up. It had a fireplace, a king-size bed with a four-poster frame and a chest of drawers with a big mirror. The furniture was golden oak and very appealing with the rich burgundy brocade coverings on the bed. The color was echoed in the draperies and the area rug on the hardwood floor. It didn't look lived in but it looked comfortable. Chastain looked up at Philippe with wonder in her eyes.

"So is this where you wanted me to stay with you?"

He nodded. "This is it. What do you think?"

They had left their coats downstairs and she'd also taken off her shoes when they entered because she didn't want to mar the glossy floors that had obviously been recently refinished. She sat on the edge of the bed and bounced up and down a couple of times.

"This bed is really nice. I think this could work, if you still want to after what I have to tell you," she said solemnly.

He felt a slight tinge of alarm at her words. She

looked so serious he went to her to offer whatever comfort he could. "Baby, what's the matter? You're acting so strange," he told her as he put his arms around her.

"It's because I've had a very strange day. I'll tell you all about it, but first I have to tell you how sorry I am," she said in a whisper.

Her words weren't reassuring in the least. "Sorry for what?"

She looked into his eyes and put one small hand on either side of his face. "I never thanked you for buying the triptych," she said. "I should have said something right away and I didn't. I acted like it was no big deal and it really was a big deal, the biggest. You helped support me and our city and I'm so grateful, Philippe. I didn't want you to think that it was just a meaningless gesture…"

She finally stopped talking because he kissed her. Once his mouth touched hers words became superfluous. He was hungry for her and the fire that always blazed between them only served to increase his desire.

Chastain kissed him back, sucking at his lower lip and using her tongue to excite him more and more. She gradually pulled away from him, insisting that they had to talk.

"No, we don't," he said as he took off his suit coat. "We don't have to say a word."

She looked tempted but unconvinced. "Philippe, there're so many things I have to tell you I don't know where to begin. We really need to have a talk," she insisted.

Philippe was sliding her jacket off her shoulders as she talked. "How about a compromise," he said persuasively. "You can talk about anything you want for as long as you want as long as we're both naked."

She laughed. "Are you kidding?"

"Not at all," he assured her and stood up to remove his shirt and pants. "I'm way ahead of you, you'd better catch up."

She looked up at him and sighed. "Fine. If that's the only way I can get you to listen, I'll take my clothes off."

She stood up and took off her camisole, revealing a strapless black lace push-up bra. "May I have a hanger, please?"

He got her one from the closet and watched her put the camisole on it, topped by the jacket. She unfastened her trousers while asking if he had a hanger for her pants. He handed it to her and watched in fascination as the pants slid down her legs, revealing a black lace garter belt and matching thong. The garter belt was attached to silk stockings that made him feel like he was sweating inside.

While she folded the slacks carefully at the crease, he watched her elegant sexy body move. "Hot damn, Cerise. How long have you had those?"

"I started wearing them when I was in Paris. You like?"

"I love. I changed my mind about naked. Leave those on," he said.

In seconds they were in the big bed. He was naked

and throbbing and she was clad in the wispy underwear that felt as good next to his skin as it looked to his eyes. They were face-to-face, wrapped up in each other's arms. She was not only pressed against his erection, she was moving her hips in the familiar, provocative way that drove him crazy.

"Okay, you wanted to talk, Cerise. Go ahead and talk," he said, his voice heavy with desire.

She put her hands on his chest so that her soft palms were rubbing his nipples in circles. Her eyes were locked on his and her hips were moving in a smooth rolling glide that made rational thought next to impossible.

Her fingertips replaced her palms and she increased the pressure on the most sensitive parts of his chest, raking her fingernails over them until they were as hard as bullets. She replaced one hand with her mouth and her hips were moving more and more as her legs opened wider. He put his hand between her thighs and felt the moisture. The warm liquid let him know that she was just as aroused as he was, if not more. They moved of one accord so that she was on her back and he was on top of her. He pushed the delicate black lace to one side and entered her in one smooth stroke. Her legs went around his waist and the feel of the silk hose heightened the experience for him. The presence of the thong increased the friction and helped them both achieve a shattering, urgent climax.

The bra became a casualty of lust as he took it off and tossed it across the room. Now it was his turn to treat her breasts to sweet torture as he massaged them with his hands and rubbed the nipples with his thumbs. When they felt so hot and hard they were like big gems, he began licking and sucking while she pumped so hard it felt like a hand was squeezing his manhood.

Their mouths fused together and with their tongues doing a slow dance, their bodies couldn't be satisfied. The garter belt was the next to go, and the silk stockings and the thong. Now there was nothing between them but a fine sheen of perspiration that made their bodies slide against each other as he thrust into her over and over again. He was moving slowly, so that the long hard length of him was rubbing against her wet jewel and making her orgasms more intense. He kept up the pace until a sudden movement of her pliant body made him go faster and faster until the pressure made him explode and her taut pelvis helped suck him until he was saying her name over and over and over. It was a long time before either one of them had a word to say.

They were still naked an hour later, after the pulsing and throbbing slowed down and they were able to breathe again.

"Did you have something to tell me?" Philippe said, trying to sound innocent.

"You're hilarious," she murmured. "I do have to talk to you, but first you have to tell me that you accept my apology."

Philippe held her closer, "I thought that was pretty

apparent. Besides, I've told you a couple of times to quit apologizing to me. I know how you feel, Cerise."

"You think you do," she replied, "but that doesn't mean I don't have to say it. I want you to hear the words from my mouth. And you don't seem to realize that I'm a woman of infinite mystery. You may not know as much as you think."

"Oh, yeah? What do you think I don't know about you?" He sounded content and amused.

"Well, I may have a father out there after all," she said. "When Tippy told me he died before I was born she exaggerated slightly. He did a disappearing act and since he was dead to my mother, he was dead to her, too. And there may be a slim chance that my mother is out there somewhere, also," she said, choking a little.

"What do you mean, Cerise?" The amusement left his voice and there was only concern for her.

"I mean that my mother left New Orleans when she was pregnant with me and came back after I was born. I was less than a month old," she said, sounding close to tears. "She left a few days later, left without me. She was only seventeen, Philippe. Can you imagine?"

"No, baby, I can't."

"After she left nobody ever heard from her again. They looked for her, looked high and low and hired a detective and everything. Tippy said her heart was smashed to pieces by my father and she never got over it and that's why she left in the first place and why she dumped me and took off again. And it's also why she made you dump me," she said dully.

Philippe made a growling sound in his throat. He stroked her face with his long fingers. "Cerise, I didn't dump you. I admit that what your grandmother said influenced me to tell you that you should date other people when you went off to college, but it was never my intention to break up with you. I was trying to do the right thing for you, baby. I didn't want you to have to settle for me without knowing what else was out there," he said.

"That's what Tippy said. She said I was being mean to you and I needed to get over myself."

"She didn't say that, did she?"

"Yes, she did. Not word for word, but what she said was close to it. After you broke my pitiful little heart she kept saying that you were all wrong for me because you were a rich boy who couldn't possibly love someone like me. Her heart was in the right place, I guess, because she felt like she was saving me from the family curse of teenaged pregnancy. She was sixteen when she had my mother and my mother was seventeen when she had me and since I was being Little Miss Hot Pants with you, she figured a great-grandchild was on the way any day. She did what she did out of love, but damn, Philippe." Her voice trailed off and she was quiet.

"There's no 'but', Cerise. I'm not going to pretend like I was happy with the way things turned out, but suppose we hadn't been separated? Look at everything you would have missed out on," he said.

She brought her body up so that she was braced

against his chest, looking down at him with all the love she felt shining out of her teary eyes. "I am, Philippe. I'm looking at you," she said with a little sob.

"Aww, don't cry, Cerise. I hate to see tears in your eyes. We're together now and that's what matters." He was going to say more when her cell phone rang.

"With my luck it's probably Tippy. Who else could have such horrible timing?"

It was indeed her grandmother. Chastain was trying to sound like she wasn't lying naked in bed with a man, but Tippy couldn't have cared less, apparently.

"Baby girl, I'm at the loft," she said in a very perky and carefree voice. "I'm going to bed so I'll see you tomorrow, okay? Don't forget we're getting out early tomorrow. Sleep well," she added before disconnecting the call.

"You didn't say much," Philippe observed.

"I couldn't get a word in edgewise," Chastain said. "She told me she'd see me tomorrow. Can you imagine?"

He laughed and said, "We'd better not waste any time then. Come here, baby."

She tossed the phone aside and went into his open arms.

Chapter 19

Chastain truly resented having to wake up the next morning. Philippe was singing to her, which normally would have been endearing, but when he was blasting her eardrums out with his deep voice, she wanted nothing more than to stuff a sock in his mouth. He was singing "This Christmas" and she had to grudgingly admit that he had a fine voice.

"Philippe, I love you more than my next breath but if you don't shut the hell up I'm going to punch you in the mouth," she told him. "Why are you bellowing in my ear?"

"Because you have to hit the shower, honey, so you can get ready to hit the road with Miz Lucinda. Antoine is taking her on a personal tour of the Food Network and he's going to introduce her to all kinds of people. He's so crazy about her he wants her to appear on his show when they start taping it," he said.

Chastain was amazed. "How do you know all this?"

"Because while you were sleeping, Ricki called me and Miz Lucinda called me and they were both quite chatty."

She didn't want to move because he was spooned against her and the heat of his body felt so good she couldn't bear to break the connection. The decision was made for her when he rolled away from her with no warning. The next thing she knew he was standing next to the bed with the covers in his hand and she was freezing.

"Don't play, Philippe. You know how mean I am in the morning," she said crossly.

"Oh, yeah, mean as a baby kitten. I just got back on your grandmother's good side and I'm not screwing it up." He was talking to her back because she had dashed off to the shower to get warm again.

The bathroom had a big old-fashioned claw-footed tub and a hand-held shower with about twenty settings. Chastain was playing with it when he joined her. "I just assumed you'd want company," he said.

By way of answer Chastain set the shower head to a gentle pulse and aimed it at his penis.

"Yes, I did want company. I have a new toy and I wanted to show it to you," she said, laughing.

"Just remember, baby, you started this," he warned her.

He allowed her to get him wet all over and then

lather him from head to toe. She took a long time with his manhood, using her supple fingers to massage him and pleasure him at the same time. She rinsed him carefully and gave him a look of total seduction. She kneeled in front of him and followed the pulsing warm water with her mouth until he was at a point of no return. She was concentrating on giving him the ultimate in passion until he decided it was time to reciprocate.

He brought her to a standing position and changed the speed of the shower so that he could get her wet and soapy. He used his fingers to explore the treasures between her thighs. The soft bubbles and the soft sweetness of her femininity were intoxicating, but the look on her face when her body responded to his touch was much more arousing to him. He rinsed her off with a cascading spray and followed it with a hard pulsing one that he used between her legs until he knew she was satisfied. Afterward she was ready for more but he wrapped a big towel around her and said no.

"I told you, Miz Lucinda is waiting for you and I ain't gonna be the one that makes you late."

She walked back to the bedroom and looked at her underwear with dismay. "I can either put this back on or go commando," she said. "Why didn't I wash these out last night?"

"Because you were too busy making me your love slave. Luckily, I happen to have something for you. It was supposed to be part of your Christmas present, but I think it would be more practical right now."

He handed her a pretty shopping bag and she looked in with a big smile. "I love presents," she confessed. "Philippe, this is so pretty! Thank you," she said as she took the bra and panties out of the bag. They were made of champagne colored silk trimmed in brown lace and she knew two things. One was that he'd paid way too much money for the set, and two, she'd look fabulous in it.

By the time she was dressed, albeit in the suit she'd worn the night before, he was also ready to go in a charcoal gray suit, a pearl-gray shirt and a silk tie with a paisley print. She wanted to start kissing him again but she knew where that would end up. They couldn't share a cab since he was going one way and she was going another, but he insisted on paying her fare. She was about to get stubborn about it but Philippe reminded her they didn't have time. "You can take it out in trade later, Cerise. I'll see you tonight," he added.

She was halfway back to the studio when she realized why she was smiling so hard. Part of it was that Audrey Hepburn feeling, like Holly Golightly after a night on the town. But the real reason had everything to do with Philippe and nothing else. If she could wake up with him every morning for the rest of her life, she'd be more than happy.

"Where's Mona?" Chastain asked as she took off her evening suit. "And what have you done with Lulu?"

Tippy shrugged as she went through Chastain's closet. "She had some errands to run, I think. She went out a little while ago. That big handsome James took Lulu for a walk. He said he wanted to see if she could help him pick up women. Wear this, baby. I like this color on you."

"She better not recruit any chicks for him," Chastain answered. "Veronica will beat him like he stole something if he looks at another woman. She has big plans for him, although I'm not sure he's aware of it at the moment." She agreed with her grandmother's choice of a honey-colored cashmere tunic. She added skinny jeans, brown boots, the big necklace she'd worn to the opening show and an angora beret that matched the tunic. "Okay, I'm ready," she said.

"Not without some makeup, you aren't. You can take five minutes to put on some mascara and some lipstick. And I know you're not going out without perfume," Tippy chided her.

She was right as usual and with the addition of a mere five minutes to her breakneck routine, she had added her grandmother's suggestions along with a light misting of Caleche.

"Now you're ready to go, *cherie*. You look very fine."

"And you look fabulous," Chastain replied.

The elevator went down, and she smiled. "That's probably James and Lulu," she said. "Did my baby miss me last night?"

"She must have because she wouldn't get in that hooker-looking bed," Tippy laughed. "She slept with me."

Lulu barked as soon as she saw Chastain. James was

carrying her and he put her down on the floor. She ran to Chastain and demanded her attention.

Tippy gave him an arch smile. "So, did you meet some women?"

James looked mortified. "No, but a couple of men seemed mighty interested in both of us. I'm sorry, Chastain, but I'm never taking her out again. She apparently gives the wrong impression to people."

Tippy couldn't resist the urge to meddle. "That's a good thing, sweetie. I think Veronica might not appreciate other women fawning over you," she said coyly.

Chastain rolled her eyes as she got Lulu's treats out. She went into the bedroom and fed her a few pieces before putting the rest in the crate. "I promise I'll be back soon. And if I'm not here, Mona will be, okay? I have to go before Tippy scares poor James to death with her nosiness."

She said the same thing to Tippy as they got into the car that Antoine had sent for them. "You really just have to mess with people's love lives, don't you? Why did you say that to James? Veronica might not have wanted him to know."

"Of course she does. Did you see the smile on his face? That was good news to him, baby girl. He likes her as much as she likes him. I'm not messing with people. I'm helping them do the right thing, that's all."

She sounded so smug that Chastain wanted to rattle her. "If that's the case, tell me my father's name. I think I have a right to know."

To her surprise Tippy gave her a calm, serious look.

"You do, Chastain, but I'm not going to be the one to tell you. That's something you're going to have to hear from someone else."

Chastain was stunned into silence. She'd expected almost anything from her irrepressible grandmother, but never that. It wasn't even on the list of answers she thought she'd get, but she knew without being told that Tippy wasn't going to change her mind.

The evening's festivities at Studio L went way beyond Chastain's expectations. The weather, in her opinion, was quite foul and she didn't think there would be a good turnout, but she was wrong. Not only were the attendees plentiful, they were rather high-caliber. She was surprised to see well-known athletes, actors and TV personalities in the crowd.

"How did all these people end up coming tonight? I'm not unappreciative, I'm just surprised," she murmured to Philippe, who was right by her side.

"You can probably thank Ricki for some of it. She's a professional fundraiser and she's really good at it, too. She knows everybody on the east coast and people just love her. I'm sure she's been on the phone for a few days."

"That was so sweet of her, Philippe. I feel like I've known her forever. How did I manage to not meet her when we were growing up? I mean, you're cousins and she had to have come to visit at some point," she said.

"Ricki and I were talking about that one day. Paris

usually went to Atlanta for the summer and you were gone to Baton Rouge or Shreveport, so there were times when her family was in town and you weren't and vice versa. And her mother's people are from Cape Verde and they would go over there for the summer or up to Massachusetts where they have a lot of relatives."

It wasn't just the attendance that was making the event so successful; it was they way everything was working together. The zydeco band was so good it was like listening to the late great Clifton Chenier at Tipitina's, one of the best clubs in New Orleans. The food could have come out of the kitchen at Tippy's restaurant. It tasted just as authentic as any in the Big Easy. Best of all, though, was the fun the family was having.

Toto and Toot were in their element. They enjoyed the music and food, but they really enjoyed the endless array of women with whom they could flirt. Tippy was the real belle of the ball, though. She talked and flirted and charmed her way through the crowd and everyone thought she was amazing, especially Chastain.

"I hope I can be just like you when I grow up," she teased her.

Tippy went serious on her again, cupping her face with her hand. "Don't ever wish that, baby girl. You stay just like you are, sweet and loving. Promise me that won't change, you hear me?"

Chastain agreed at once, although she was once again mystified by her grandmother's abrupt change of demeanor. She forgot about it quickly enough when she was doing her own meeting and greeting and receiving accolades on her art. At some point she missed Mona, who had disappeared from the party. She'd barely glimpsed her all night, which was strange.

Once the auction was over and the amazing amount of money raised was applauded, the crowd began to thin. Before the band left Toto and Toot were prevailed upon to sing with them and they did so gladly and very well. Chastain looked at Tippy and said, "You know, they could be there all night. The band is going to want to leave shortly."

"I can fix that, honey." Tippy went over to the band stand and beckoned to Toot. He leaned down and she whispered something to him. He got a huge grin on his face and sliced his finger across his throat to signify to Toto to stop.

"My friends, we have a special request from a very special lady. There is someone here with a really good voice and I have it on good authority that he's more than willing to sing, because if he doesn't, he's going to donate a thousand dollars instead. Come on up here, Mr. Deveraux."

Chastain was shocked by her uncle's words but she was stunned when Philippe said he'd be glad to. He had a fine baritone voice, but he wasn't prone to advertising that fact. He wasn't the kind of man who just burst into quasi-spontaneous song and then laid on the false modesty when people started swooning. She was ready to write the thousand-dollar check herself just to make it all go away, but he seemed perfectly at ease.

"This is something I may never do again and I've

had just enough to drink to make it seem like a good idea, so bear with me," he said. When he started singing "You Were Always on My Mind," Chastain had to dig her nails into the palm of her hand to keep from weeping. She was trying to be at least somewhat dignified but she was failing miserably. Tears were rolling down her cheeks when he looked at her with the same tenderness as the words he was singing. Ricki was next to her and Chastain was glad she had her shoulder to hold on to because her knees were buckling.

When it was over, he thanked everyone for their wild applause and said, "By the way, I'm still giving that donation. The song was for someone very special."

Chastain didn't even try to front. "Tippy, Lulu and I are going with Philippe. I'll see you in the morning," she said.

"Well, I should hope so, honey. Be good," she said, "or be good at it. And leave Lulu here with me. She'll be just fine."

Chapter 20

After her folks went back home, Chastain moved most of her things into the brownstone. The very thing she said she wouldn't do, she was doing with the speed of light. She wanted to spend every possible minute with Philippe because she loved him and because she felt it would be more respectful to David. She wasn't vain enough to think that she was the love of his life or anything, but she wasn't trying to rub his nose in her affair, either. Besides, she was missing a roommate.

Mona spent more time away from the loft than in it. She was still doing a good job of assisting Chastain with her appointments, but she was spending her downtime somewhere else. Chastain was pretty sure she knew why and she teased her about it.

"So who is this dreamboat and why haven't you brought him over for an inspection," she said sternly.

She was packing a few things with Lulu's supervision and Mona was lingering around the doorway. She jumped guiltily when Chastain made her playful statement.

"What? Oh, that," she said coyly. "He's someone I've known for a long time."

"A college sweetie? That's fun, why don't we all have dinner or something?" Chastain was surprised to see Mona blushing.

"This must really be serious," she said. "Okay, when you're ready to introduce him to me, we'll do dinner. I hope it's before Christmas, though. We're leaving on Tuesday," she reminded Mona.

Mona went from looking mildly amused to looking dejected. "I keep forgetting you're going to New Orleans for Christmas," she said wistfully.

"I'm really excited about it, too. I can't wait to see the rest of my family and Philippe's, too. Tippy actually suggested that I bring David with me to introduce him to my cousin Janelle." She gave a horror-movie shudder, complete with sound effect. "I told her I might not want to be with David, but I wasn't trying to set him up, either. Janelle is one of the most annoying people you'll ever meet in your life. I wouldn't subject a nice man like David to her." Mona gave her a vague smile in return.

"Are you feeling well, sweetie? When are you leaving for D.C.? Because you can leave anytime you want to. I know you want to get home for the holidays and I can handle anything that comes up between now and when Philippe and I leave."

She was shocked when Mona's only response was to give her a big hug. "You're so thoughtful," she said. "I'm going to miss you."

Chastain hugged her back. "I'm only going to be gone a week or so. I think it's Lulu you're really going to miss." She grinned. "She's going to miss you. You're the one who shares her toast every morning and who rescues her from her crate. But we'll be back."

"I still don't think you should drive all that way," Mona said as she played with Lulu's ears.

"It's not that bad a drive. Philippe is renting a nice van and we're leaving early enough to take our time. I just don't want Lulu to have to ride in the cargo hold. I promised her she'd never have to do that again after we came back from France. It's the least I can do for my baby," she said cheerfully. "I've got enough stuff, I guess. I'll see you tomorrow," she added as she put on her coat and clipped Lulu's leash to her harness.

Mona mustered up a smile as they were leaving, but Chastain noticed it wasn't her usual happy one. "Mona, I'm telling you, if you're not feeling well go home early. If you were to hop on a train tonight I couldn't blame you. You've been working really, really hard and you deserve to take it easy. Let me know if you need anything."

"I will, I promise," Mona assured her. "You get going because the snow is kicking up something awful out there."

Chastain made a face. "That's the one thing I won't miss about New York. We don't have all that nonsense back home."

Even though it was a temporary residence, the brownstone felt like a home to Chastain. She was surprised at how much she liked being there, but the truth was she would have enjoyed being anywhere with Philippe. He surprised her by bringing her a stack of holiday DVDs and CDs. She had a surprise for him, too: she had bought a slew of Christmas decorations in Mardi Gras colors. There were white lights, gold, green and purple ornaments and bows and, just for Lulu, a bunch of little white dogs. There was also an angel for the top of the tree. It was ridiculously corny, but the evening they spent trimming the tree and watching *A Charlie Brown Christmas* and *The Preacher's Wife* was going to be one of her favorite memories.

Tonight she was cooking for him, something she hadn't had a chance to do in years. She made jambalya and served it with a green salad and crusty French bread. She also had a bottle of wine chilling. Now that she knew there wasn't a history of alcoholism in her family, she was going to try it.

Lulu was in her usual spot on the window seat in the living room when she started to whine and paw at the glass. That meant she'd seen Philippe. They both ran to the door to greet him.

"Wow. What a homecoming. Do I get this every night?"

"If you're good to us, yes, you do," she crooned before kissing him.

It was supposed to be a quick peck, but very little was quick where Philippe was concerned. He liked to kiss and he liked to take his own sweet time, lavishing her lips with his love.

"Let's go upstairs," he said.

"After dinner. I made you something really good," she told him.

He kissed her again, longer and harder and told her, "You're all the goodness I need. Can't we heat it up?"

"That's what you're doing to me right now," she said, "but no, we're not heating it up. It won't taste the same. Wash your hands and we'll have dinner and you can have whatever you want for dessert."

He gave her the seductive smile that made her nipples do a happy dance in her bra. "You're on, Cerise. It smells fantastic, whatever it is."

She took his overcoat off his broad shoulders and went to the closet to hang it up. "You'll see," she said. "Wash your hands and meet me in the kitchen. And Lulu has already been out, so don't listen to her heinous lies."

He played with Lulu for a few minutes before going into the downstairs powder room to wash up. He followed his nose to the kitchen and Lulu followed him. His eyes lit up when he saw the heavenly concoction she'd prepared.

"Chastain, this looks just like I remember it. You cook so well you could have been a chef if you wanted to. You're an artist in the kitchen, too."

"You're so sweet to say that, Philippe."

He gave her a stern look. "There's nothing sweet about telling the truth." After he took a bite his eyes closed in gratitude. "This is better than I remember. You're a culinary goddess, baby."

They enjoyed the meal with jokes and laughter and Chastain had a new experience; her first glass of wine. It was more like a half glass, but she found it to her liking. "This is like white grape juice but really good grape juice." She licked her lips and smiled. "So this is what all the fuss is about. I can see why people like it."

"I still can't believe that Miz Lucinda told you that alcoholism ran rampant in your family."

Chastain laughed. "She should have said that nutti-ness runs in my family because it does. She had me convinced that half of our people were either hopeless drunks or AA zealots who'd seen the light. It would have been a lot more to the point to have a little talk with me about the perils of drinking and let it go, but that's not her style." She looked deep in thought for a moment, and then she made a face.

"Philippe, suppose I turn into Tippy? We've got the same blood, I could end up just like her, meddling in people's lives and messing with their heads," she said in a voice that was slightly horrified.

"It's absolutely impossible, Cerise. You'll never be anything but the fantastic woman you are. You're never going to change. You've been the same way since the day I met you and I don't ever want to think about you not being you. I can't imagine such a thing."

She was so touched by his words she couldn't say a thing.

Chastain had taken a long hot shower when she got to the brownstone so she waited for him downstairs. She was curled up on the sofa with Lulu watching *A Christmas Story* and she was a little bit sleepy. She made a mental note to remember that wine had a soporific effect on her. Philippe called to Lulu from upstairs and she went to him with the speed of light. Chastain still maintained that Lulu loved him best, but who could blame her? He was wonderful.

In a few minutes he came downstairs, wearing a robe and a smile. He had two bath sheets with him and a couple of towels. "You're not asleep are you? I remember you saying something about dessert."

She returned his smile with one of her own. "I'm not sleepy in the least. I was just conserving my energy." She made a graceful move with her arm and removed the soft warm throw she'd been covered with and revealed a sexy red bra that fastened in front with a satin bow. The matching panties were worn low on the hips and barely had enough material to cover her essentials. The result was hotter than fire. Philippe was so entranced by what he was seeing that he walked into the upholstered coffee table.

"You need to warn a brother when you're going to do something like that. Suppose I had a bad heart or something?"

Chastain rose to a kneeling position and tried her best to look innocent. "It's a good thing you don't have a bad heart because I may owe you dessert but you owe me for the other morning when you were rushing me," she reminded him. "Where's Lulu?"

"She should be asleep by now after the bribe I gave her. The door is closed so she won't be joining us. And I thought I'd more than made up for the other day but I'm happy to kick it up a notch if you so desire."

"What are you doing?" she asked.

"I'm setting the stage for seduction," he answered. He had covered the coffee table with the two bath sheets and put one of the towels on top of them.

She admired his ingenuity; the table was long and wide and so sturdy that it was very difficult for even a grown man to move by himself as they had found out the previous day when he tried to move it in front of the fireplace. He did it anyway and it was now in front of a crackling fire. Once he was finished with the towels he straddled the table and held out his hand to Chastain.

"Come over here, baby. Santa's got something for you."

"Wait just a minute," she said. "I want to turn off the lights."

It took her just a moment to turn off all the lamps and the room was bathed in firelight and the soft twinkle of Christmas lights. Using the remote, she turned on the CD player which had a holiday compilation disc loaded. Chastain started singing along to

"Santa Baby" in her husky contralto voice and doing her best bump and grind walk as she returned to Philippe. Since she'd learned the art at Toot's show bar, she'd learned how to do it right. She ended the song kneeling between his thighs for a kiss.

"Miss Thibodaux, you amaze me."

"Back atcha, baby. Since you serenaded me I think it's only fair that I sing to you. Kiss me."

Philippe was more than happy to oblige her. Her soft juicy lips never failed to send his temperature up and with it his libido. They were kissing wildly, but as they kissed he was lifting her up so her legs could rest on top of his. He held her waist and guided her body until she was on her back. The kiss was finally broken but only because Philippe loved to look at her. He untied the satin bow between her bra cups and smoothed the silky material aside so he could feel her breasts. They were just the right size, just like everything else about her.

He lavished her breasts and the sensitive spot between them with his tongue before he began to seek out her hidden sweetness. He was removing her sexy panties while he was making his way down so that she was completely naked, laid out like a sensual new land for him to discover. Her skin glowed bronze in the firelight and the look of love on her face made the love he was feeling for her surge even higher. She had a little surprise for him. At some point she'd trimmed her soft curly patch into a neat little heart shape. He massaged her mound with both hands, using his thumbs to allow him more access in order to maximize the sensation for her.

Once his tongue touched the honeyed tenderness her hips began moving, slowly and delicately and then faster and more urgently as the steady stroking of his tongue made her insides quiver and melt like ice cream. He cradled her hips as he explored every bit of her, licking and sucking her until the juices flowed over his lips. When the trembling aftershocks began to slow down and her breathing returned to normal, he urged her into a sitting position so they were facing each other with her legs over his. She looped her arms around his neck and gave him the smile he loved.

He had long since taken off the robe and the fire-light made him look like burnished gold. His hands were around her waist, holding her close to him.

"Are you thirsty?" he asked.

"Not so much," she said.

"Hungry?"

"Yes," she said, nodding her head.

"What would you like?"

She placed her hands on his broad shoulders and lifted her hips so he could enter her. "This is just what I wanted," she whispered.

"And it's just what I want you to have, baby. All of it."

She locked her legs around him and they pushed and pumped until their sweat-slicked bodies came together in an explosive orgasm. It was hard to say who made the most noise but they really didn't care. All that mattered was that they were both so, so satisfied.

Chapter 21

Lucien looked at his twin brother and smiled. "Philippe, I'm impressed. You said that as soon as Chastain was back in the country you were gonna rope and hog-tie her if you had to and damned if you didn't do it."

The two men were in the living room of Lucien's house. Philippe was holding his niece, Courtney. She was almost three and absolutely fascinated by the fact that she now seemed to have two daddies. She kept looking from Lucien to Philippe and laughing. Lulu was being chased through the house by Yum-Yum, one of the puppies from her only litter. They ran into the dining room and stared each other down for a minute and then Yum-Yum took off so Lulu could chase her.

The house was decorated for Christmas and it was a truly domesticated scene.

"Go easy on the rope and hog-tie thing," Philippe advised Lucien. "It was just about that bad for a minute. I saw those damned pictures and I went off on her so of course we were going at it pretty good for a few days. But we worked it out. Nothing was going to keep me from her for very long. We're part of each other."

Courtney was cuddled in his lap and she clapped her hands every time the little dogs ran by. Between the dog races and the two daddies, she was in heaven.

"However it happened, I'm just glad it did. It's about time you two settled down and got serious about each other."

"You're right, for a change. It doesn't happen often, but even a broke clock is right twice a day," he laughed.

"You got jokes, huh. Old, stale corny jokes, but you got 'em."

Courtney was starting to look sleepy and Philippe asked if he should take her to her mother. Lucien looked insulted.

"Excuse me, but I am quite capable of putting my baby to bed. You need to come observe because I have a feeling you and Chastain are gonna uphold the Deveraux tradition of big families."

"You have a point. Let's go. Move, man, I can carry her up the stairs without dropping her. I'm not exactly unskilled with babies, thanks to our fertile cousins."

"Just watch where you put your big feet, there's

bound to be dog toys or baby toys underfoot some-where."

"I can handle it if you just move out of the way."

Chastain was in the kitchen with Lucien's wife, Nicole. Nicole was eight months pregnant and counting down the days until she delivered.

"I love my husband and I adore my daughter, I truly do. But at a certain point you just get tired of being pregnant. I'm past that point right now," she admitted.

"Aww, you poor thing. I have no idea what you must feel like. Would you like me to rub your feet or give you a pedicure? Would that help?" Chastain asked.

"You're very sweet to offer, but believe it or not, Lucien rubs my feet for me every night. He also rubs my tummy with vitamin E oil and cocoa butter and I love it. He's always attentive but he's just amazing when I'm pregnant. But don't worry, I'm sure that Philippe will treat you like a queen, too. Have you two set a wedding date?"

Chastain moved her head from side to side to indicate no. "The subject of marriage has not reared its head," she said dryly. "Living together is present and accounted for, but marriage is out there in the strato-sphere somewhere with all the other impossible dreams."

Nicole looked shocked and quickly tried to adopt a more neutral expression. "Maybe he's just assuming that the marriage is inevitable. He's famous for keeping his business private. Until I saw you two kissing at my wedding reception I had no idea that you two were an item," she reminded Chastain. "No idea whatsoever and you know I like to be the first one to know any kind of juicy gossip."

Chastain was busy wiping the condensation off her glass of iced tea with her fingertip. "Maybe we won't get married. Marriage doesn't seem to be on the agenda for Thibodaux women."

She had told Nicole all about Tippy's revelations, including the fact that the father she'd believed to be dead was in all probability very much alive.

"Look, all I have to do is call Titus and he will be on it," she said firmly. "If he's out there, Titus will track him down in no time." Her brother Titus Argonne was one of the best-known and most successful investigators in the country and she wasn't joking when she said he could find anyone.

"I'm not ready to do that," Chastain said. "I may not ever be ready to do that. When he found out my mother was carrying me his family sent him off to California and he never looked back. If he wanted anything to do with me he could have contacted me years ago and he didn't, so why should I bother?"

Nicole's eyes were full of sympathy. "Hey, I'm adopted so I know about feeling conflicted about birth parents and all. I never wanted to look for mine because my adopted family is all the family I could ever want or need. Titus actually asked me if I wanted to find them and I looked at him like he was crazy. If you ever want to know who the guy is, just say the word."

Chastain finished drinking her tea. "I'll keep that in mind." Lulu and Yum-Yum skittered into the kitchen panting as if they'd run a marathon. Yum-Yum went to her water bowl and Lulu looked at Chastain reproachfully.

Nicole laughed. "I know that look. If you don't mind, could you look under the sink for another water dish? Lulu looks like she's about to perish from thirst."

Chastain filled the bowl and gave it to a grateful Lulu. Philippe entered the kitchen with a satisfied smile.

"I just bathed my niece and put her to bed," he said proudly. "Lucien said I did it perfectly, too. However, I don't think Courtney is going to go to sleep without a song from her mommy."

Nicole got up with a grin. "That's our daily routine. We must have a song before sleep. I'm going to say good night because once I get upstairs I'm not coming down again. I'll see you tomorrow." She hugged her friend and gave her brother-in-law a kiss on the cheek.

Philippe was still bragging about his baby wrangling prowess after they got home. Philippe had a big restored house in the Garden District and she was staying with him. She loved his house. The rooms were big and there were plenty of closets. The kitchen was a dream to cook in because he'd had it redone a few years ago. All the bathrooms had been redone, too. One of her favorite parts of the house was the back porch, which was screened in and lent itself to privacy. But she was also fond of the balcony off the master bedroom.

They had debated about putting up Christmas decorations since the holiday was so close and they would only be there for a week, but ultimately they decided to go for it. He bought another potted pine tree and she bought more decorations and they managed to pull off a festive look.

"We're going to have to do brunch or something while everyone is here," he said.

She agreed. "Tippy wants everyone to come for Christmas Eve at Mama T's. Maybe we can do a day after party if no one has anything planned."

The week would be a round of parties and gatherings with his folks and hers. She was looking forward to all of it but she was dreading the inevitable question that seemed to be on everyone's lips: "So when are you two tying the knot?"

She wanted to know the answer to that one herself and it didn't seem like he was in any hurry to discuss it. But there were many times when she didn't care if he ever brought it up. He was kind and caring, he treated her like she was royalty, and he was an incredible lover and a wonderful human being. He made her laugh, he comforted her when she was sad and he would truly have done anything for her, so the piece of paper was just a formality. And when she drifted to sleep in his arms it wasn't even that. It was just a piece of paper.

Chapter 22

Chastain looked at Philippe over the rim of her coffee cup. "I haven't heard from Mona," she said.

"At all?"

"Not a word," she said distractedly. "I told her to go ahead and leave early for the holidays because she wasn't feeling well. I was kind of surprised when she just up and left the next day without saying anything to me, but that was cool. Or I thought it was until I realized she'd taken everything with her."

"She cleared out all of her things, not just things for a week at home?" Philippe was sounding concerned, too.

"She didn't leave so much as a dust bunny," Chastain confirmed. "And now I can't get her on her cell phone or by e-mail. I've left messages but I get nothing back. I hope she's all right. She was more like a friend than an assistant."

"I know that, baby. Maybe she went out of town with her father. If you haven't heard from her by the time we go back to New York, I'll get Titus on it."

She nodded forlornly. Philippe couldn't stand to see her unhappy.

"Apparently we're hosting the day after brunch for family and friends. If you feel like making a grocery list we can go shopping for provisions," he said.

She smiled at him and reached over to take his hand. "I know what you're doing. You're trying to make me forget that I'm worried by keeping me busy."

"Yes, I am. I admit it, that was my master plan. Is it working?"

"It will. I'm going to make that menu right now and we can go out this afternoon. The stores are going to be horrible," she warned him.

"Hey, you're forgetting who you're talking to. If I can bathe a slippery baby I can manage a grocery cart. We'll be in and out of that store so fast it'll make your head spin. Trust me, Cerise, we got this."

Christmas Eve at Mama T's was a long-standing tradition. Since the extended family was so large, it was easier to have a big party at the restaurant. This way friends, family and people with no place to go could have a good meal and a lot of fun. It was always the best party in town, but this year it would be even better as far as Chastain was concerned, because Philippe would be there with her.

She wanted to help cook, but Tippy said she would be in the way. "We've been doing this so long it's like a science, baby girl. All you have to do is show up looking pretty."

Chastain didn't even have to help with decorations or setting the tables because Tippy's efficient staff handled that. The party was in the main dining room. The tables were pushed together so that there were two long tables and everyone would be served family style. Tippy always provided an amazing array of food, everything from the traditional goose with chestnut stuffing to gumbo. Or turkey and dressing to crabmeat *étouffé*. Anything anyone wanted could be had at Mama T's on Christmas Eve.

One nice thing about the event was that there was no dress code. There was no need to be formal, but if that's what made a person happy, it was just fine. All manners of attire were acceptable from sequins to over-alls. Chastain had planned on wearing jeans so she could help serve but when that was vetoed she decided to smarten up her act a little.

Philippe was running mysterious errands so she took advantage of his absence to shampoo her hair and take a long hot shower. After she toweled herself off she took out her jar of Magie Noire body cream and rubbed in on every inch of her body. For once she didn't have to shoo Lulu away from licking her legs while she applied the cream because she was off with Philippe.

After her body was moist and scented all over, she blew her hair dry and used a big curling iron to give it lift and body.

She painted her toenails and fingernails, something she didn't do very often because her hands often had paint or charcoal all over them. She kept her nails short and shaped and now they sparkled with a thin coat of sheer gold polish. Next came her makeup and it wasn't her usual five-minute application. She took time to apply eyeshadow to her eyelids using a metallic bronze on the lid and champagne under the brow, followed by several coats of mascara. The end result was stunning, even to her critical eye. She normally skipped blush, but she applied a little bronzing powder to accent her cheekbones.

She decided to wait until Philippe came home to get dressed. There was no point in lounging around letting her outfit get wrinkled. While she waited for his return she put on some Christmas music and sipped a glass of white wine mixed with club soda. She had on her fancy underwear that Philippe had given her and her favorite robe, a silk charmeuse kimono from the Paris flea market. Curled up on the sofa listening to Aaron Neville sing "O Holy Night," Chastain felt utterly content.

Philippe came in with two shopping bags and Lulu. He put the bags in the dining room and came over to kiss her.

"Why are you sitting in the dark, Cerise?"

"I didn't really notice," she admitted. "I was daydreaming and I lost track of time." Lulu had joined her on the sofa and was trying to lick her ankle. "Hurry up and get showered and dressed," she said. "I've been waiting for you and I'm starving."

"Give me about twenty minutes and I'll be ready," he promised.

He was true to his word, too. He showered quickly and got dressed in a pair of navy trousers and a navy cashmere sweater. By the time he came downstairs again Chastain had put on her outfit. It was one she'd purchased in Paris and never worn. The top was a light-weight cashmere sweater with cap sleeves and a deep scoop neckline both in front and back. It was a champagne color that looked fabulous against her skin and she wore a short skirt in the same color. The skirt had inverted pleats under the high waistline and it accented her figure beautifully. She dabbed on some gold lip gloss and slipped on her gold slingback pumps and she was ready.

Philippe looked at her as if he wanted to say forget the party, let's stay home. "You look exceptionally gorgeous tonight. I don't know what I did to deserve you."

She laughed, but he looked very serious. "Let's go, sweetheart. I'm hungry and so is Lulu."

He kissed her on the forehead and stroked her neck with his long fingers. "Anything you say, baby."

The party was as good as Chastain knew it would be. There were six Christmas trees around the restaurant, decorated in red, gold, green and purple with white lights. Pots of white poinsettias were displayed as well and the dining room looked very festive. Everyone she knew and loved was there and it was wonderful to see everyone. She hadn't seen some of the guests in ages so it was like a homecoming for her.

Philippe's father was there with his lovely wife, all of Philippe's brothers and their wives, with the exception of Wade who liked chasing women too much to settle down. His sister, Paris, was much too pregnant with twins to make the trip from Atlanta, but Philippe said they could go visit Paris and her family before they went back to New York.

Chastain's family was there in full force, her great-uncles, her uncles and their wives and children, plus her many cousins. The food was good and so was the music. Lulu was enjoying herself in spite of the fact that Chastain kept her on her leash so she wouldn't run around and get lost. Even the best times have to end, though, and Chastain was about to suggest they call it a night when she realized that Philippe wasn't by her side. She looked around and finally saw him holding a microphone at the bandstand.

"Friends, neighbors, family, if you could all hold it down for a minute, I have something to say. A long time ago I fell in love with the most captivating woman I've ever met and I love her even more today. I have something to ask her if she'll come up here with me."

Chastain wasn't sure how she got to where Philippe was standing because her legs felt like they weren't going to hold her up. Somehow she made it all the way to his side while everyone cheered and clapped and whistled. Everyone got quiet once she was next to Philippe and he put his arm around her waist.

"Chastain, I can't possibly live without you and I hope that you will be my bride so I can devote my life to making you as happy as you make me. Do you think you can do that?"

"Absolutely. I can't think of anything else I'd rather do," she told him.

He slipped a ring on her finger and they kissed to the delight of everyone. Tears were glistening in her eyes as he held her but the tears turned to laughter as Lulu broke away from Lucien and raced over to join them.

It was much later when Chastain actually got a good look at her engagement ring. It was a five-carat solitaire that Philippe said was a cinnamon diamond. "It was my grandmother's. If you don't like it, we can get something else," he assured her.

"Don't be crazy, I love it. I love you," she said as she kissed him again. They were at home and she was looking at her ring in the light from the fire.

"I'm glad you love it and I'm real glad you love me because I love you more than my next breath. That ring has been waiting for you for a long time, Chastain."

"What do you mean?"

"I had to go pick it up from my safe deposit box today. Here's the box and here's the receipt for the change in settings. See the date?"

She had to blink back her tears again because it was dated December 2005, the Christmas she'd told him about the fellowship. She looked at him and he confirmed what she was thinking.

"I had the ring and I was going to give it to you on Christmas Eve because it just seemed romantic. Then you told me about your grant and I didn't want to stop you from pursuing your dream and I didn't propose."

"Philippe, the only reason I took the damned grant was because you hadn't proposed! If I'd known you wanted to marry me I wouldn't have put a foot outside of Louisiana. We could have been married with three children by now."

"You want some babies? We can have as many as you want. Twins run in both our families, so we should be able to have a horde of them. Little girls that look like you."

He wiped away a tear than was running down her face. "Why are you crying?"

"Think about all the time we wasted," she said.

"I'm thinking about all the time we have, baby. We'll have a lifetime together."

"That sounds so good, Philippe. You're the only man I've ever loved."

"And you've always been my girl. Let's get married on New Year's Eve. What do you think?"

"Yes! Absolutely yes," she said happily.

Lulu gave a bark of approval, before she turned around three times and went to sleep. She had better things to do than watch them kiss.

Chapter 23

Chastain couldn't remember when she'd enjoyed the holidays so much. She couldn't even remember a time when she hadn't loved Christmas. That was the magic of the love Philippe lavished on her. He had made all her bad memories vanish and he'd replaced them with new ones, ones that she would treasure always. She still loved looking at her ring and he would always smile when he saw her doing it because she looked so pretty and flushed with love whenever he caught her staring at her ring finger.

"I can't seem to stop myself. This is the most beautiful thing I've ever seen. I don't have a lot of jewelry." She blushed and corrected herself. She had more now that she'd ever had. Philippe had given her the beautiful oval diamond in its custom setting for their engagement. But for Christmas he'd given her diamond studs for her ears in a star-shaped setting, another gold necklace, this time with a diamond pendant, and five gold bangle bracelets. He had a knack for picking out things she would adore. He also gave her a gift set of Magie Noire and one of Chanel No.5, lingerie and a gift card to the best art supplier in New Orleans.

She'd lavished him with gifts, too, just because she wanted to. She'd given him a beautiful silk robe in navy because she liked him in that color. She also gave him a book full of pictures she'd drawn of him over the years, along with a note that told him the nudes were his to do with what he wanted. She gave him a black cashmere sweater and two dress shirts with matching silk ties, but she also gave him a couple of really nice sweatshirts because she didn't want him to lose his edgy style completely. She also gave him the Eckhart Tolle books and a gift card for more books.

They both gave Lulu presents, a new leash and harness, chew toys and a snappy striped sweater. The best gift of all wasn't under the tree. He gave her carte blanche to decorate their home any way she liked.

"Whatever you want to change, change, Cerise. I want you to be happy here when we move back."

He had given her some news along with her Christmas gifts. The president wanted him in Washington for three months and he was actually concerned that she might not want to go.

"Of course I do, sweetie. I love D.C., but more importantly, I love you and I never want to be away from you again. Lulu will like D.C., too, won't you?"

Lulu barked once and then she yawned, as if to say she didn't care where she was as long as she was with her humans.

Chastain was sitting in her favorite place, Philippe's lap. They were in the living room on the sofa watching the rain and Lulu was curled up tight against his thigh. She kissed his neck and inhaled the fresh, clean scent of his skin.

"We should be making wedding plans," she said. "Instead of necking like teenagers, we should be doing something productive."

"We're doing something productive," he countered. "We're solidifying our bond, how does that sound? Between Mom and Miz Lucinda we're not going to be allowed to do anything but show up, so let them roll with it."

The postman rang the bell and Chastain got up to answer the door. It was a priority mail envelope postmarked New York with Studio L's return address. She went back to the living room to open it. Inside was a letter from Mona with a Post-It note from Veronica.

I thought you might want to see this ASAP. Happy Holidays, V.

She went back to Philippe's lap and leaned on him while she opened the letter. Her eyes widened and her hand went to her mouth as she read. Philippe sensed her anxiety and asked her what was in the letter.

"I'll read it to you," she said.

"Dear Chastain,

"I know you're wondering why I bolted off and haven't taken your calls or returned your texts or e-mails. It's because quite simply, I've been living a lie. After I met your grandmother I couldn't do it anymore.

"I know you think that we met by accident, well that was the first lie. I went to Paris to seek you out. I'd been following your career on the Internet and through art magazines and I read about your genius grant, so I went to France. I made it my business to get to know you and to become your friend. I didn't want anything from you except friendship because I knew I had no right to ask for what I really wanted, which was for you to know that I am your sister.

"We have the same father, Winston Morgan. He was the man who ran away after finding out that your mother was pregnant with his child. When you came to Howard University, he saw you on campus when he was doing a speaking engagement. He says he recognized you right away and it almost gave him a heart attack because you looked so much like your mother.

"He kept an eye on you after that. He didn't feel as if he could ask you to be a part of his life since he had ruined his relationship with your mother so badly. But I really believe that he cares about you, even though he had no way of show-ing you that he cares. He couldn't contact you directly, partly because of his career and partly because of his wife, my mother.

"I know this reads like a bunch of excuses to you and I'm sorry. I thought what I was doing was harmless until your grandmother pointed out the serious repercussions that could come from what I was doing. I truly didn't mean any harm. I just wanted to get to know my big sister in the hopes that one day you could accept me as a sister. When your grandmother met me she knew exactly who I was because of my resemblance to my father. As she put it, you never forget the face of the man you hate.

"I hope you don't hate me and I hope that one day we can be friends. I hope that you will be more gracious than I have been and accept my sincere apology.

"Mona"

Chastain looked at the letter the same way she would have looked at a piece of junk mail and put it back in the envelope. She handed it to Philippe and said, "Would you file that for me? I don't want to deal with it right now." Her voice was soft but very cold.

"What do you want to do, darling?"

"Get married."

"Then that's what we'll do and we won't deal with this until you're ready."

"Fine by me. Let's go bug your mom and then let's go bug Tippy and then let's see if Nicole has any more of that sweet potato pie. I need to be with my family, my real family."

"That sounds like a plan, all except the part about the pie. Lucien is a fiend for sweet potato anything and the chances of there being any left are slim to none."

"Oh. Well we'll get some at Mama T's or I'll make one. I just have a taste for it."

Philippe hid his smile. She might call it a taste, but he was pretty sure that she was having a craving. He suspected that their first child was growing inside Chastain, even though she wasn't aware of it yet. He couldn't wait until they knew for certain so they could celebrate the joy of starting their family.

As far as the family she may or may not have had, he was going to protect her and support her in any way that she needed him to until she was ready to deal with the situation. Of course, he was also going to give his brother-in-law Titus Argonne a call. It never hurt to be prepared, he thought as he looked at the beauty in his arms. He made a mental note to call Titus that very night.

Ten years.
Eight grads.
One weekend.
The homecoming
of a lifetime.

PASSION OVERTIME

PAMELA YAYE

As homecoming festivities heat up, PR rep Kyra Dixon is assigned to nab pro football star Terrence Franklin as Hollington's new head coach. Kyra knows the sexy star well… intimately, in fact. Kyra and Terrence were once engaged… until he dumped her for football dreams of glory and groupies. Now they've got some unfinished business to resolve—the business of seduction.

Hollington Homecoming:
Where old friends reunite…
and new passions take flight.

HOLLINGTON HOMECOMING

KIMANI ™
ROMANCE

Coming the first week of November 2009
wherever books are sold.

In December, look for book 4 of Hollington Homecoming,
Tender to His Touch by Adrianne Byrd.

www.kimanipress.com
www.myspace.com/kimanipress

KPPY1371109

REQUEST YOUR FREE BOOKS!

2 FREE NOVELS
PLUS 2 FREE GIFTS!

KIMANI™
ROMANCE

Love's ultimate destination!

YES! Please send me 2 FREE Kimani™ Romance novels and my 2 FREE gifts (gifts are worth about $10). After receiving them, if I don't wish to receive any more books, I can return the shipping statement marked "cancel." If I don't cancel, I will receive 4 brand-new novels every month and be billed just $4.69 per book in the U.S. or $5.24 per book in Canada. That's a savings of over 20% off the cover price. It's quite a bargain! Shipping and handling is just 50¢ per book.* I understand that accepting the 2 free books and gifts places me under no obligation to buy anything. I can always return a shipment and cancel at any time. Even if I never buy another book from Kimani Press, the two free books and gifts are mine to keep forever.

168 XDN EYQG   368 XDN EYQS

Name	(PLEASE PRINT)
Address	Apt. #
City	State/Prov. Zip/Postal Code

Signature (if under 18, a parent or guardian must sign)

Mail to **The Reader Service:**
IN U.S.A.: P.O. Box 1867, Buffalo, NY 14240-1867
IN CANADA: P.O. Box 609, Fort Erie, Ontario L2A 5X3

Not valid to current subscribers of Kimani Romance books.

Want to try two free books from another line?
Call 1-800-873-8635 or visit www.morefreebooks.com.

* Terms and prices subject to change without notice. Prices do not include applicable taxes. Sales tax applicable in N.Y. Canadian residents will be charged applicable provincial taxes and GST. Offer not valid in Quebec. This offer is limited to one order per household. All orders subject to approval. Credit or debit balances in a customer's account(s) may be offset by any other outstanding balance owed by or to the customer. Please allow 4 to 6 weeks for delivery. Offer available while quantities last.

Your Privacy: Kimani Press is committed to protecting your privacy. Our Privacy Policy is available online at www.eHarlequin.com or upon request from the Reader Service. From time to time we make our lists of customers available to reputable third parties who may have a product or service of interest to you. If you would prefer we not share your name and address, please check here. ☐

KROM09

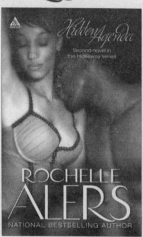

HELP CELEBRATE
ARABESQUE'S
15TH ANNIVERSARY!

ARABESQUE®

2009 marks Arabesque's
15th anniversary!

Help us celebrate by telling us about your
most special memories and moments with
Arabesque books. Entries will be judged by
the Arabesque Anniversary Committee
based on which are the most touching and
well written. Fifteen lucky winners will
receive as a prize a full-grain leather duffel
bag with the Arabesque anniversary logo.

How to Enter: To enter, hand-print (or type) on an 8 ½" x 11" plain piece of paper your full name, mailing address, telephone number and a description of your most special memories and moments with Arabesque books (in two hundred [200] words or less) and send it to "Arabesque 15th Anniversary Contest 20901"—in the U.S.: Kimani Press, 233 Broadway, Suite 1001, New York, NY 10279, or in Canada: 225 Duncan Mill Road, Don Mills, ON M3B 3K9. No other method of entry will be accepted. The contest begins on July 1, 2009, and ends on December 31, 2009. Entries must be postmarked by December 31, 2009, and received by January 8, 2010. A copy of these Official Rules is available online at www.myspace.com/kimanipress, or to obtain a copy of these Official Rules (prior to November 30, 2009), send a self-addressed, stamped envelope (postage not required from residents of VT) to "Arabesque 15th Anniversary Contest 20901 Rules," 225 Duncan Mill Road, Don Mills, ON M3B 3K9. Limit one (1) entry per person. If more than one (1) entry is received from the same person, only the first eligible entry submitted will be considered. By entering the contest, entrants agree to be bound by these Official Rules and the decisions of Harlequin Enterprises Limited (the "Sponsor"), which are final and binding.

NO PURCHASE NECESSARY. Open to legal residents of U.S. and Canada (except Quebec) who have reached the age of majority at time of entry. Void where prohibited by law. Approximate retail value of each prize: $131.00 (USD).

VISIT **WWW.MYSPACE.COM/KIMANIPRESS**
FOR THE COMPLETE OFFICIAL RULES